The Forbidden Chest

The Famous JUDY BOLTON *Mystery Stories*

By MARGARET SUTTON

In Order of Publication

THE VANISHING SHADOW
THE HAUNTED ATTIC
THE INVISIBLE CHIMES
SEVEN STRANGE CLUES
THE GHOST PARADE
THE YELLOW PHANTOM
THE MYSTIC BALL
THE VOICE IN THE SUITCASE
THE MYSTERIOUS HALF CAT
THE RIDDLE OF THE DOUBLE RING
THE UNFINISHED HOUSE
THE MIDNIGHT VISITOR
THE NAME ON THE BRACELET
THE CLUE IN THE PATCHWORK QUILT
THE MARK ON THE MIRROR
THE SECRET OF THE BARRED WINDOW
THE RAINBOW RIDDLE
THE LIVING PORTRAIT
THE SECRET OF THE MUSICAL TREE
THE WARNING ON THE WINDOW
THE CLUE OF THE STONE LANTERN
THE SPIRIT OF FOG ISLAND
THE BLACK CAT'S CLUE
THE FORBIDDEN CHEST
THE HAUNTED ROAD
THE CLUE IN THE RUINED CASTLE
THE TRAIL OF THE GREEN DOLL

"She's still alive, Peter, but we'll need help!"

"She's still alive, Peter, but we'll need help!"

A Judy Bolton Mystery

THE FORBIDDEN CHEST

BY

Margaret Sutton

Grosset & Dunlap

PUBLISHERS   NEW YORK

COPYRIGHT, 1953, BY
GROSSET & DUNLAP, INC.

ALL RIGHTS RESERVED

PRINTED IN THE UNITED STATES OF AMERICA

The Forbidden Chest

*For the Western
Branch of the Family
at Wild Wolfe ★ Ranch*

Contents

CHAPTER		PAGE
I	An Interrupted Story	1
II	Judy Is Curious	10
III	"Curiouser and Curiouser"	17
IV	Peter Tells a Secret	27
V	Holly Is Accused	34
VI	A Real Mystery	43
VII	A Nagging Doubt	51
VIII	After the Accident	59
IX	A Possible Clue	67
X	A Valuable Collection	75
XI	A Disrupted Plan	82
XII	A Strange Coincidence	90
XIII	Stranger Still	98

Contents

CHAPTER		PAGE
XIV	More than Coincidence	107
XV	Horace's Headlines	114
XVI	An Underground Adventure	122
XVII	A Dangerous Risk	131
XVIII	Judy's Plan	139
XIX	Destination Unknown	146
XX	The Prison Car	154
XXI	A Full Confession	163
XXII	At Wild Horse Ranch	174
XXIII	Questions and Answers	185
XXIV	When the Chest Was Opened	192
XXV	A Borrowed Birthday	200

The Forbidden Chest

CHAPTER I

An Interrupted Story

"This is it, Judy! Number 12 Oak Street. I hope Cousin Cleo is at home."

Judy Bolton, now the young wife of FBI agent Peter Dobbs, stopped the car in front of the house her new friend, Holly Potter, had pointed out. All the blinds were drawn.

It had been a pleasant drive from Dry Brook Hollow, through Farringdon where the two girls had stopped for luncheon with Judy's mother, and on along the main highway to the quaint Pennsylvania town of Wyville. But it had taken a good two hours.

"I'm afraid we've made this trip for nothing. It looks as if your cousins have gone out," Judy said.

The Forbidden Chest

"If they have, I'll get my stuff anyway," Holly said. "They expected me to come back for it."

She banged the knocker. Then she shook the knob of the front door.

"It's locked, Holly," Judy told her.

"Oh, well! There are other ways of getting in. Come, I'll show you."

Still the same red-haired, adventure-loving girl she had always been, Judy followed her companion eagerly. The side entrance was also locked, but this did not stop Holly. Pulling over a lawn chair, she climbed up on it and produced the door key from a ledge overhead.

"See what a good hiding place this makes? Cousin Cleo always keeps the key over the door. Cousin Fred doesn't like to carry it around with him. He loses things," Holly explained. "Besides, when I came home from boarding school unexpectedly, it was awfully handy to know where to look for the key."

"It might be handy for burglars, too," Judy laughed.

"Burglars! In a little town like this?"

"I didn't mean to alarm you," Judy said quickly, seeing the look of fear that crossed Holly's face. "I'm so used to working with Peter on FBI cases that such possibilities just naturally enter my mind. Crime isn't limited to big cities, you know. I could tell you about crimes that have been committed in towns even smaller than Wyville."

"I'll bet!"

An Interrupted Story

Holly turned the key in the lock, and the door swung open upon a neat service entrance just off an immaculate kitchen.

"Enter!" she invited with an elaborate bow.

She laughed, but there was a sober look in her eyes that Judy noticed.

"Does it seem a little strange—coming back here?" she asked the younger girl.

Holly was silent and Judy began to fear her question had stirred up too many memories. Holly had not been happy living with her cousins. After the death of her parents, they had taken her from a sense of duty, and afterwards placed her in a near-by boarding school. A plain, shy little girl, Holly had not made friends. When Judy first befriended her, the troubled fifteen-year-old had said gratefully, "Judy, I feel closer to you in one day than I did to any of the girls in boarding school in all the time I was there."

The two girls were becoming good friends, although Holly's moods would always puzzle Judy. Now, Holly answered her question abruptly.

"Yes, it does seem strange. It always did. You may think this house is beautiful, but it never seemed like home to me. Home isn't a show place. It's being with people you care about. I never cared for my cousins, and I never will. The people I'm going to live with are the ones who matter—my uncle and my sisters. Cousin Cleo shouldn't have separated us."

"You're still bitter about it, aren't you, Holly? I know it was hard," Judy sympathized, "but thanks to my dear black cat and the clue he provided, the misunderstandings are all cleared up. And your cousins have tried to make things right since then. It's too bad they're not here to greet you."

"They'll probably be back before I've finished gathering up my stuff. I should have brought something to pack my things in," Holly added, "though there won't be much to pack. This way, Judy. My room's upstairs."

"Wait a minute!" Judy protested. "Don't rush me through this beautiful dining room."

"It *is* nice, if you like antiques," Holly admitted as Judy stopped to look around. "The glassware you see on the window shelves is Cousin Cleo's pride and joy. But I've always felt like a bull in a china shop here. Once I broke one of her Dresden teacups and I don't think she's ever forgiven me. Those are Majolica plates on the wall."

"They're lovely, but that sparkling colored glass in the window is simply out of this world," declared Judy. "It must be priceless."

"I guess it is," Holly admitted. "I know I was never allowed to touch it. That blue glass hen dish on the top shelf used to tempt me, but now I think I like the paperweight best."

An Interrupted Story 5

"What paperweight?" asked Judy.

"It's in the living room on Cousin Fred's desk. Cousin Cleo says it's a Millville Rose. Come and look at it," Holly invited, and led the way into the living room. She drew Judy over to the window and put the paperweight into her hand.

"Hold it yourself and then look," Holly said. "You don't see the beauty of it until you look down into it the way you'd look down into a pool. There! Now can you see inside the glass?"

"Ah, yes!"

Judy could see very well, and what she saw nearly took her breath away. At first the large, deep red rose in the center had seemed to be the only flower in the weight. But now, as she watched, a swirl of green leaves and stems spread out from a bubble at the base of the rose. Altogether there were six of the bubble-like stems with a flower at the end of each one. The flowers seemed to be morning-glories and were so delicate in coloring and design that they appeared almost translucent.

"This is exquisite," declared Judy as she replaced the paperweight on the desk. "I've heard of the famous Millville Rose, but not in a bouquet. This combination of roses and morning-glories must be extremely rare."

"Yes, I'm sure it is," agreed Holly. "Cousin Fred says unusual weights like this were never sold. They were made at the end of the day out of left-over bits of glass, and were given as presents. I used to pretend that the glass blower gave this one to his little daughter, Felicity. I don't know where I heard the name, but it's always enchanted me. It means *happiness*. Somehow, the paperweight seems out of place—here."

"I don't think so. It goes with everything else. I've seen rooms not half so attractive as these on magazine covers," declared Judy. "My grandmother left me a few antiques along with the house in Dry Brook Hollow. Maybe I could show them off to better advantage. Do you think your cousin Cleo would mind if I borrowed some of her decorating ideas?"

"Oh, Judy! Not *her* ideas," begged Holly. "You and Peter would be miserable in a living room like this. What good are beautiful things that nobody can touch or use?"

"I see your point," Judy admitted.

She could tell without touching them that many of the ornaments in the living room were fragile. A china clock adorned the mantel over the fireplace. It was decorated with angels and pale pink rosebuds almost as delicate as the flowers in the paperweight. Apparently the clock was in running order as it ticked steadily. The hands pointed to three.

"We ought to start back by four o'clock," observed Holly. "And it will probably take me an hour to sort my

An Interrupted Story

things and pack them. Let's go upstairs. My clothes are in the guest-room closet. It is good of you to help me, Judy," Holly added warmly. "I'm going to love having you for a neighbor."

"It will be mutual," Judy assured her, following her upstairs. "Dry Brook Hollow will never seem lonely again with you and your sisters living on the farm right next to ours. When Peter's away on his mysterious trips I'll just ask one of you over—"

"Me, I hope."

Holly stopped suddenly, eyeing a tall secretary that stood in a corner of the room they had just entered.

"I left a story in the top drawer of this thing. I just remembered it. Oh, good!" she exclaimed as she opened the drawer. "Cousin Cleo didn't throw it away. Want to hear it?"

"I'd love to hear it!" exclaimed Judy, sitting down on the bed to listen. Holly had told her she hoped to be a famous author some day, but Judy had yet to hear one of her stories. "Is it very long?" she asked as the younger girl opened a thick ruled tablet.

"No, it was going to be, but I never finished it," Holly explained. "I started it on New Year's Eve. I was home—I mean here—for the holidays, and everyone else was out, so I just sat up and wrote until midnight. It was fun."

"Was it?"

"Of course. I didn't even know I was alone. You don't, Judy. Not when you're making up people. I made up Felicity first."

"Felicity? But that's what you called the glass blower's daughter."

"I know. She's my heroine. I was going to call my story 'The New Year' and have it be the year 1880. That was going to be the year Felicity's father is forbidden by his company to make any more paperweights. It is a terrible blow to him. It just about kills his creative art. I had it all written that way, and then I looked it up in the library and—Judy, you won't believe this, but it *was* that way. The last paperweight was made at Millville in the year 1880. It was uncanny. I couldn't finish the story. My pencil started shivering all over the paper."

"I should think so," agreed Judy. "Maybe you've lived before—as Felicity," she suggested, smiling.

She said it in fun, but Holly took her seriously.

"That's just what I thought. How else would I know? I mean, if I hadn't lived before as—as someone else."

Judy laughed reassuringly.

"Maybe you have a sixth sense or something. What I can't understand is why the men were forbidden to make paperweights."

"Because they used the company's glass gatherings. I seemed to know that, too. Anyway, in the story, Felicity is alone when the man comes to tell her father

An Interrupted Story

about the new rule. She is writing her New Year's resolutions."

"What are they?"

"You'll find out when you read the story," Holly promised. "They're real resolutions. I found a page torn from an old diary. In January, 1880, someone really did make ten resolutions just like Felicity's. One is not to be afraid of anything, but she nearly jumps out of her skin when a thunderous knock sounds on the door of her father's house."

Judy gave a start as a loud thump sounded on the door downstairs. Holly's story was almost *too* realistic.

"Good gravy! Someone *is* knocking!" Holly exclaimed, handing Judy the tablet. "Here, you read the story while I go down and see who it is."

CHAPTER II

Judy Is Curious

DOWNSTAIRS Judy could hear Holly demanding in a shaky voice, "Who's there?" and then, after an inaudible reply, asking more sharply, "Why didn't you ring the bell? That knocker makes an awful noise."

"I didn't see any bell," was the sullen answer.

"Well, come in if you're the regular boy. I'll see if Cousin Cleo needs any."

This was Holly's voice again. Judy's curiosity got the better of her and she tiptoed to the head of the stairs. She could not see the boy himself. But she could see his reflection in the big mirror over the living-room fireplace. If he had glanced up he might have seen her

Judy Is Curious   11

reflection, too. But his eyes were riveted on the rose paperweight, which he was holding in his hand.

"He's just a boy. Probably he doesn't realize how valuable that paperweight is," thought Judy.

The covered basket over his arm indicated that he was selling something—possibly bread or rolls. Her curiosity satisfied, Judy returned to Holly's room and became so absorbed in the story her friend had written that she paid no more attention to what was going on downstairs.

"This is wonderful!" she exclaimed when Holly reappeared a little later. "I love your heroine, Felicity. She's amazingly like you, though. You're not going to leave her feeling, as you say here, that she is the rose imprisoned in the glass, are you?"

"I don't know. How far have you read?"

"Just up to the part where Felicity hears the knock. That was uncanny, too."

"I know," agreed Holly. "That's the way things keep happening to me—just as if they'd happened before. I told you I couldn't finish the story. Maybe the rest of it will come to me some time."

Holly spoke hurriedly. She seemed to be searching for something.

"I hope I'm around to read it when it does. By the way," Judy asked, "who was that boy at the door?"

"Just an egg boy," Holly replied. "I went to see if Cousin Cleo needed any eggs, but she has plenty. The books I had downstairs are all ready to go and here's an old suitcase that will do for my clothes. Judy, would you mind packing them for me? We haven't much time."

"Of course," agreed Judy, glad to help. "Shall I pack the story, too?"

"You may as well, though I'll probably never finish it. I don't have the right feeling for it any more," confessed Holly. "Felicity seems real, but none of the other characters do. I can't make them modern. That spoils it, somehow. And it's hard to imagine what real people did back in 1880. They couldn't go to the movies or listen to the radio or watch television. Girls had so little freedom, I should think they would have felt like prisoners. But maybe I made Felicity feel that way because I did, and still do, when I'm here. The— the atmosphere or something is all wrong for me. Come on, Judy. Let's get out of this house. It's given me the creeps already. Put the story on top of my clothes if you want to. I don't think there's anything else to go except the chest."

"What chest?" asked Judy.

Holly did not answer. She was already clattering downstairs. Judy packed the story, picked up the suitcase, and followed her down the stairs. But she stopped halfway. Again the mirror over the fireplace showed her what was going on in the living room. Holly was attempting to move a large brass-covered chest.

Judy Is Curious 13

"Wait and I'll help you!" called Judy. "That chest looks heavy. Have you packed your books in it?"

"In *this* chest?" asked Holly in evident surprise. "Oh, no! It's forbidden."

"Forbidden? But why?"

"I don't know," the younger girl returned mysteriously. "Lots of things in this house are forbidden. This chest is *mine*, though."

Holly made this last statement as though she expected someone to deny it.

Judy looked at the chest more closely. It was covered with what looked like hand-hammered brass in an intricate design of wreaths and dancing figures. A circle of holly leaves adorned the hinged cover which was now secured with a small padlock. In the lock was a tiny brass key.

"Are you going to open it?" Judy asked.

For a moment Holly just looked at her. Then she said in almost a whisper, "I wouldn't dare!"

"What are you going to do with it?" Judy persisted.

"I'll take it along without opening it and throw my books in the luggage compartment of your car. That is, if there's room for them after we get this chest in there. Do you think it will fit?" questioned Holly.

Judy eyed the chest doubtfully. It would fit all right. That wasn't the problem.

"Holly, are you sure you ought to take it?" she began. "It looked so pretty in the living room where your cousins had placed it, and if you aren't sure—"

"But I am sure," Holly interrupted. "I don't know what's in it, but it's mine and it will look nice in my study. You said you'd help me with it," she hurried on before Judy could protest any further. "I don't want to mar Cousin Cleo's polished floors by dragging it over to the front door. We'd better take it out that way. It will be quicker."

Judy agreed, although she still doubted the wisdom of taking it.

"I'm curious," she confessed. "If this chest were mine, I wouldn't be satisfied until I found out what was in it. When are you going to open it?"

"Maybe I never will."

"Oh, Holly! That's absurd. Of course you'll open it sometime. That space by the wall looks awfully empty without it. Don't you think you ought to leave a note or something to explain things?"

"Well, okay, if it will make you feel better."

Opening the suitcase, Holly tore a page from the back of the tablet containing her story and scribbled hastily:

Dear Cousins:

You were out when I came to get my things. The key was over the door where it always is, so I went in and took only what was mine. Judy came with me. She has to get back before dark, so we couldn't wait—

Judy Is Curious 15

"I don't mind waiting. I really think we ought to wait a little longer," Judy said.

"We can't," insisted Holly. "It'll take us two hours to drive back, and I have to be home by six. You know how my uncle is about wanting his meals on time. By the way, you're invited too."

"Thank you," said Judy. "I will stay if they expect me. Peter may not be home until late, so I wasn't going to prepare anything."

"Well, let's go. I'm starved already," declared Holly.

She ended her note with a brief *"Thank you,"* signed it, and propped it up on the mantel beside the angel clock. Then she turned to Judy.

"There! Does that satisfy you?" she asked.

Judy laughed.

"It doesn't satisfy my curiosity, if that's what you mean. But I guess I can stand it a little longer."

"Come on, then," urged Holly.

Judy picked up the suitcase and Holly followed her to the car, her arms full of books. She deposited them on the back seat and the two girls returned for the chest.

"You take one end," Holly said, "and I'll take the the other."

"Holly, wait! Where's the rose paperweight?" cried Judy. "That beautiful one you showed me! It's gone from the top of the desk!"

16 The Forbidden Chest

"It is!" Holly exclaimed in surprise. "I'm sure it must be around somewhere," she said, glancing about the room. "Maybe I moved it by mistake when I was collecting my books. Some of them were on the desk."

"I hope it wasn't stolen. I didn't like the way that egg boy was looking at it," declared Judy. "He could have slipped it into his basket. I noticed that he kept the basket covered."

"It had eggs in it, and eggs break if you aren't careful of them. I'm surprised at you, Judy," Holly said, giggling, "suspecting an innocent egg boy. The paperweight's here somewhere. Come on, let's hurry!"

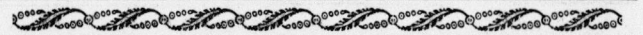

CHAPTER III

"Curiouser and Curiouser"

IT WAS a hard struggle down the front steps with the chest, as there was no way to get a good grasp on it. Judy could tell that the chest was not empty. Something rattled inside when they put it down as gently as they could in the luggage compartment of the car. Judy looked at Holly in dismay.

"What was that?"

"I don't know," Holly said. "Maybe we've broken something. How do we know what precious stuff may be in it?"

"We don't," Judy said, really curious now. "This chest has me mystified. If your cousins forbade you to look in it, what makes you think you have the right to take it?"

"Because it's mine. Anyway, they didn't," Holly

replied even more mysteriously, and ran around to the back of the house to replace the key over the door ledge.

"Not a very safe hiding place," remarked Judy when Holly was beside her in the car. "I hope nobody saw you put it there."

"Who would?"

"I don't know. It's just strange—about that paperweight, I mean. And I don't believe in inviting trouble," declared Judy, "but I'm afraid that's what we're doing —taking the forbidden chest and whatever that was rattling around inside it."

"It's all right. Don't worry about it," Holly assured her easily.

Still Judy couldn't help wondering about the chest. Its presence in the car made her drive even more cautiously than usual and Judy was a careful, if not an experienced, driver. Peter had taught her to drive. Whenever he could spare the car, she used it. Today Peter was working on a case with his immediate superior, David Trent. Judy was curious about that, too, but she never questioned Peter. If there was anything she could do to help him in his work, he would tell her when the time came. Meanwhile, she could help Holly. And she had to admit that the chest and its contents puzzled her more and more, the more she thought about it.

"Let's just forget the whole thing," Holly replied

when Judy questioned her for the dozenth time. "If you're my friend, you'll trust me to do the right thing."

"I do," declared Judy, "but you can't blame me for being curious."

"Curiosity killed the cat."

"Oh, Holly!" exclaimed Judy. "That one has whiskers. Curiosity never killed Blackberry," she added with a laugh. "He's poked his nose into plenty of mysteries, too."

"A regular G-Cat," agreed Holly. "The first and only!"

Holly was one of the few people who knew Peter was a G-man. To most of Judy's neighbors he was a young lawyer who had given up his office and taken some sort of selling job. That explained his frequent trips. Judy, of course, had been known as a girl detective from high school days. Solving mysteries had been her hobby even before the Roulsville flood, when she and her brother Horace had been offered the so-called haunted house in Farringdon as a reward for their heroism. That house had provided plenty of chilling adventures. Later, the house she inherited from her grandmother had provided still more baffling puzzles, and Peter's work as an FBI agent had added to the list. As Horace had teasingly remarked, "Judy without a mystery to solve is like apple pie without the cheese."

Judy, smiling, told Holly of her brother's remark. She glanced back toward the chest, and Holly said,

"Judy, you're hopeless. You're as bad as the girls in fairy stories who are always stealing a look at forbidden things. Don't you ever wonder what would have happened if they hadn't looked?"

"I don't have to wonder," Judy said. "I know. There wouldn't have been any story."

Holly gave up and they talked of other things. It was late, and as they entered a stretch of woods, a number of startled deer looked up and fled from an orchard where they were grazing. A bunny hopped across the road, then another and another.

"I'm afraid to drive too fast for fear I'll hit one of them," confessed Judy.

Holly gave her a knowing glance. Another reason was the chest, but no more was said about it until they turned down the unpaved road that led to Holly's uncle's home, where she and her two sisters now lived. Ruth, Holly's married sister, came to the door with the baby in her arms.

"Eric!" she called to her husband. "Here's Holly with her things. Will you help her bring them in?"

Eric Hansen, a hearty, good-natured, blonde young man, came out and, before Judy could protest, lifted the chest from the luggage compartment and bore it into the house without assistance.

"Careful!" warned Judy as he set it down.

Her warning came too late. This time the clank inside sounded even more like breaking glass.

"Curiouser and Curiouser"

"Holly, you'll have to open it now, to see if anything's broken," declared Judy.

Holly's sister Doris agreed.

"I've always wondered what Mother kept in there," she said. "Even when we were children I remember how she used to close the chest quickly as if it contained an important secret. Now we'll find out what it was."

"Oh, no, we won't!" returned Holly. "This chest is mine and it's going to stay shut. I can't open it, anyway," she added. "I don't have the key."

"But Holly, it was in the lock. Didn't you take it out and put it in your pocket?" Judy asked her.

Holly shook her head.

"I didn't see the key in the lock and I don't have it, and if I never find it, that will be all right with me."

"You're hopeless!" exclaimed Doris. "What good is a chest that you can never open?"

"It's plenty of good." Holly was adamant. "I'll keep it in my study and use it as a window seat."

Holly's study, as she liked to call it, was the room back of the living room. Here she hoped to do her writing as well as her sleeping. One entire wall was lined with bookshelves.

"It gives me an urge to write just to be here," she declared.

And yet she had no urge whatsoever to find out what was in the chest. Judy couldn't understand it. Eric moved the chest, more carefully this time, and Holly promptly piled cushions on top of it and stood back to see how it looked.

"What do you think?" she asked Judy and Doris. Ruth had returned to the nursery to put the baby back in his crib.

"It looks all right," Doris said doubtfully. "Mother said it was to be yours and so I suppose you're free to do as you like with it. She must have wanted you to open it some time, though. It's too bad you lost the key, but maybe we can get a locksmith—"

Again Holly protested, not giving her pretty red-haired sister a chance to finish.

"No! This chest stays closed. Mother's last words to me were 'Don't open it!' and I'm not going to."

"Did she say why?" asked Judy.

"Not exactly," Holly admitted, "but she gave me reason enough. I was curious, just the way you are. I kept asking what was in the chest and why I couldn't open it, and finally she said, in a very serious voice, 'Because it's forbidden!' I've never forgotten it. She—she fell on her way out of the room, Judy, and after that she couldn't speak. I could never open the chest after that—never!"

Holly's voice shook. Judy could tell she was close to tears.

"Mother died of a stroke," Doris explained, dabbing

tears from her own eyes. "I've never forgotten it either. Ruth and I did what we could, but it was too late. Dad was killed overseas the same year. You know the rest, Judy—how we girls were separated, with Cousin Arlene taking me to California, Aunt Flo taking Ruth, and Holly going to live with Cousin Fred and his wife. Cleo isn't a blood relative, you know. By the way, how did you find her?"

Judy and Holly exchanged glances.

"We didn't," they both said at once. Then they laughed and that eased the tension.

"Was there trouble?" Doris asked anxiously.

Holly shrugged her shoulders.

"No. I was lucky. I didn't have to thank either of them for the wonderful home they'd given me, and kiss them good-bye, and all that. They were out."

"Oh, Holly! What did you do?"

"I just went in and got my things."

"But how could you?"

Before Holly could explain, Ruth came into the room.

"The baby's finally gone to sleep, and we're all ready for dinner," she announced. "Here comes Uncle David so there's no need to wait."

In the dining room, the old farmer whom Judy had known as a lonely recluse for the past few years, took his seat at the head of the table and bowed his head. There was no spoken prayer. Just a moment of silence during which Judy unexpectedly remembered Holly's words: "If you're my friend, you'll trust me," and her own answer: "I do."

When the conversation was resumed, Holly told what had happened at her cousin Cleo's. Holly's sisters, her brother-in-law, and her uncle all seemed to feel she had done right to go in and take her things as long as she knew where the key was.

"And I did thank them in my note. It was easier," Holly added. "I left the note beside the angel clock. Judy admired that clock."

"I admired the whole house," declared Judy. "Everything was in such perfect taste. I love antiques, and your cousins have them arranged to show them off to the very best advantage. There was a whole window full of glass, and on the desk in the living room was the loveliest paperweight—"

"The Millville Rose!" exclaimed Doris. "I remember it. Cousin Fred bought it from Mother when—when was it, Ruth?"

"That last awful year, I guess. I couldn't understand then why she sold it, but now I know. There were bills to pay. Sometimes people do what they have to do."

"Hard times," said David Potter, shaking his head. "But now all that is in the past. We're one family again. Maybe a better family than some who have had it too easy."

"Curiouser and Curiouser" 25

Judy agreed. She couldn't help wondering if she and Peter weren't a little closer, too, because of some of the hard things they had gone through together. More times than she could count, he had come to her rescue. She had been on hand, too, when he was in danger. Once she had almost lost him and had prayed for the courage to face even that.

Eager to be there when Peter returned, Judy started for home a little after nine o'clock. Her car was parked beside the road right next to the walk that went up to the Potter house. As she turned the car around, the headlights cast a wide beam of light across the walk. Something sparkled, suddenly, in the light. Judy jumped out of the car to see what it was.

"The key to the forbidden chest!" she whispered as she picked it up.

For a moment she stood there, turning it over in her hand and thinking. Should she return it at once or keep it until Holly finally did want to open the chest?

Deciding on the latter course, Judy pocketed the key, climbed back in the car, and drove home.

Although the Potters were her nearest neighbors and it took but a few minutes to run from one house to the other by the short cut, it seemed a long way around on the road. Driving down the North Hollow road, along the main highway and back through the grove to her own house, she had to cross Dry Brook twice and travel in almost a triangle. When she reached home, the house was still dark. But Blackberry was there, as always, waiting on the porch to welcome her.

"Good old Blackberry!" Judy whispered into the cat's soft fur as she picked him up and carried him into the house.

Later he followed her upstairs when she put the key she had found in the secret drawer of her dresser, and went to bed to dream of opening the forbidden chest.

CHAPTER IV

Peter Tells a Secret

"I DIDN'T hear you come in last night, Peter," Judy said to him the following morning at breakfast. "I waited for a little while with nobody but Blackberry to keep me company. Then my eyes just wouldn't stay open any longer. I wish I could remember it."

Peter smiled across the table at her.

"You're talking in riddles again, Angel. What's this you wish you could remember?"

"My dream," replied Judy, absently buttering both sides of a piece of toast.

"Was it your old favorite? The dream of floating on a pink cloud? I nicknamed you Angel after you told me that one."

Judy laughed.

"I'd make a queer angel—with red hair and freckles. No, this dream was of opening the forbidden chest."

"The forbidden chest? That sounds more like a fairy tale."

"It was like a fairy tale," declared Judy. "Holly and I had the strangest day."

"Tell me about it," urged Peter.

Judy related the previous day's adventures over scrambled eggs and coffee. She mentioned the story Holly had written, and the curious fact that she had known, before she found it in a reference book, the actual date on which certain things had happened.

"She says she feels she has lived before," continued Judy, "and her story gave me the uncanny feeling that she had, too. Could it be possible?"

"I doubt it. Physicists and others have played with the idea. It's hard to prove anything. But what about your dream?" asked Peter. "You mentioned a forbidden chest."

"I dreamed I opened it, but I don't remember what was in it. I know why I dreamed about it, though," Judy added. "It's because I'm so curious about the real forbidden chest. And I have the key."

"Then what are we waiting for? Let's open the chest. Where is it?"

Peter was as eager as a little boy.

"Holly has it," Judy told him. "She says she'll never open it, but I hope I can make her change her mind. I

Peter Tells a Secret 29

don't know when I've been so curious about anything. Think of it, Peter! She put it in her study and piled cushions on top of it, and she says she's going to use it for a window seat, though how she can sit on anything as mysterious as that chest is more than I know. She thinks the key is lost, and doesn't seem to care. But when I give it to her—Peter, if she doesn't open it then, I suppose I'll never know what's in the chest. Probably I shall die of curiosity."

"Poor Angel!" sympathized Peter.

There was understanding as well as amusement in his blue eyes.

"Maybe Holly's right and I shouldn't be so curious," Judy went on. "Some people regard curiosity as a fault, don't they? But I can't help asking myself why a chest would be forbidden, and I don't come up with any answers. I wonder—"

"Still the same 'I wonder girl' that I fell in love with," Peter said fondly. "You just aren't happy unless you have something to wonder about."

"That's true," agreed Judy. "But maybe I'd better start wondering about something else. As, for instance, where you were last night. Or is it a secret?"

"It is," declared Peter. "I'm allowed to talk about it to just one person—you!"

"Really?" Judy's gray eyes shone. "Oh, Peter! Do you mean I'm in on it officially? Does Mr. Trent really think I can help?"

"He hopes you can."

"In that case," Judy decided, "I shall forget all about Holly's chest and concentrate on your mystery. Or isn't it a mystery?"

"It certainly is!" Peter said. "A fifteen-year-old boy has disappeared. We're keeping it secret because the boy's parents are afraid it's a kidnaping. However, I'm inclined to think the boy, Harold Wilcox, has left home of his own volition."

"You mean he's run away?" Judy asked.

"It's a possibility. Fifteen is a restless age. His parents were rather vague about his friends, his interests, and a dozen other things we had to check. That's where you come in. We think maybe you can get Mrs. Wilcox to confide in you."

"Why?" asked Judy. "Wouldn't she talk?"

"She talked all right, between crying spells," replied Peter. "But she simply agreed with everything her husband said."

"And you think that's bad?" Judy inquired, smiling.

"Not for us, Angel," Peter chuckled. "But I don't think Mrs. Wilcox really agreed with her husband. Mr. Wilcox is the one who called us in on the case," Peter explained. "Although he has not yet received any demands for ransom, his wife has convinced him that the boy was kidnaped. He was seen getting into a car at three o'clock yesterday afternoon with a strange man, and that's proof enough for the parents."

"Who saw him?" asked Judy.

"Some of his schoolmates. I questioned them last night," Peter continued. "They were able to give me a fairly good description of the man. He had white hair and a little white mustache, they said. One of them told me he was rather tall and dignified-looking. The car had New York license plates ending in 20 or 002. The boys couldn't agree on that and they weren't sure whether the letter was an M or an N. Anyway, they gave us something to work on."

"Did they actually see Harold Wilcox being dragged into the car?"

Judy asked the question anxiously. She knew what a dreadful thing that was from her own experience.

"He wasn't dragged, although his mother won't believe it," replied Peter. "The boys say he got in of his own free will. He and the man seemed to be friends. One boy said he'd seen them together before. Mr. Wilcox scoffs at that, too. He's a big, blustering millionaire who seems to have his whole family intimidated. There are several grown children, some married and some in college. Harold is the youngest."

"Spoiled, I suppose?"

"Not necessarily. You're the youngest member of the Bolton family and you're not spoiled."

Judy laughed at that.

"Horace is only a year and a half older than I am. I used to think he was the spoiled one."

"This boy may have been," Peter remarked. "His home is a mansion."

"I'd like to see it," said Judy wistfully.

"You shall," promised Peter. "It's on a hilltop overlooking the Susquehanna River, and I thought we'd drive out there today."

Judy was overjoyed at the prospect of helping Peter, and began at once to get ready. There were dishes to do, Blackberry and the chickens to feed, as well as other small chores to keep her busy while Peter attended to some business in his den—the den that had once been Grandma Smeed's parlor bedroom.

"I could show off my own antiques better," thought Judy as she opened the corner cupboard to put away the dishes she and Peter had used at breakfast.

On the top shelf were a number of precious pieces of glassware and an exquisite Wedgwood plate that had belonged to her grandmother. Judy had always called it the strawberry plate because it was made to look like a basket of strawberries. She could remember eating from it just once when, visiting her grandmother, she had suddenly come down with the measles. She'd frightened everyone when her fever mounted higher and higher. When her temperature suddenly had dropped to normal, her grandmother had been so relieved that she brought in the strawberry plate heaped with real strawberries and topped with whipped cream. How delicious they had tasted! Now the plate belonged to

Peter Tells a Secret 33

Judy, but she had never used it for fear of breaking it. Maybe Holly was right when she had said, "What good are beautiful things that nobody can touch or use?"

Forgetting that she had promised herself to start wondering about something else, Judy's thoughts kept returning to Holly and her mysterious chest. Did it have glassware inside? Certainly something had clanked like breaking glass. And if it did . . . but no! She mustn't think about that chest now.

"I should be wondering about Harold Wilcox. I told Peter I would," Judy said aloud to Blackberry, who was purring around her ankles. "He's run away, or been kidnaped, and may really be in trouble. Why can't I think about him?"

"Perhaps because you don't know him!"

Peter's voice, from the doorway, startled Judy. She nearly dropped the strawberry plate.

"I intended to hang this plate on the wall, but I guess it's safer back in the closet," declared Judy. "What's that you have in your hand?"

"A photograph of the missing boy," replied Peter. "Once you look into those sad dark eyes of his, you won't be able to help thinking about him."

Judy took the photograph as soon as she had replaced the plate.

"Peter!" she exclaimed. "That boy wasn't kidnaped. I saw him *after* three o'clock yesterday afternoon, selling eggs in Wyville!"

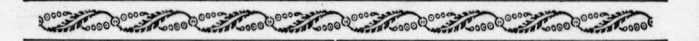

CHAPTER V

Holly Is Accused

"ARE you sure about that, Judy?" Peter questioned excitedly. "Look at the picture again. Is this the same boy you saw selling eggs in Wyville?"

"The very same," declared Judy. "I couldn't be mistaken. I recognized him instantly."

"Tell me about this egg boy."

"Well, he came to the door of the Potter house at Number 12 Oak Street just as Holly was showing me her story," Judy began. "It was the oddest thing—a knock sounded on the door in the story, and a real knock sounded on the real door at exactly the same time. That's why I was interested in Holly's caller, I guess. I stood on the stairs where I could see his reflection very plainly in the mirror over the living-room fireplace."

"His reflection?" questioned Peter. "This isn't going to be another of your ghostly mirror mysteries, I hope. Didn't you see the boy himself?"

"Well, no," Judy had to admit. "I didn't think of it before, but I saw only his reflection. He had his eyes glued on that beautiful rose paperweight I told you about at breakfast. He was holding it in his hand and he didn't even look up."

"Then how can you be sure he had dark eyes?"

"I can't," confessed Judy. "I recognized him in the picture by the shape of his face and the way his hair falls over his forehead, and his wide mouth. I *know* he's the same boy even if I didn't get a good look at his eyes. But what would a millionaire's son be doing selling eggs?"

"That's a question the boy's parents may be able to answer."

Saying this, Peter strode to the telephone and put through a call to the Wilcox mansion. Judy could hear only one side of the conversation. But she could tell the way it was going. Nobody would believe her, and yet she was sure the egg boy was Harold Wilcox. And the more she studied the picture the more certain she became. It was a school picture, not a retouched photographer's portrait. The face looked so natural, it was almost like looking at the boy himself instead of at his picture. He was even wearing the same plaid shirt he had been wearing yesterday. Judy hoped she could convince his parents when she saw them.

"What did they say?" she asked when Peter hung up the telephone.

"They didn't believe it," he replied. "Mrs. Wilcox says her boy 'wouldn't lower himself to become a common peddler,' and Mr. Wilcox doesn't think he has enough ambition. They are both sure he was not in need of money. His allowance is more than generous. Really, Angel, you may be mistaken—"

"No, Peter," insisted Judy, "I'm more certain than ever that Harold Wilcox is the boy I saw. There was the same—sort of defeated, sullen look about him. But Holly laughed when I suggested that he might have taken the rose paperweight."

"Is it missing?" asked Peter. "You didn't tell me that."

"Holly said she'd probably put it somewhere else herself," explained Judy. "I called her attention to the fact that it was gone—"

"And suggested that the egg boy might have taken it?"

"Yes."

"In that case we may have a clue," declared Peter. "However, it may be just as well not to mention the rose paperweight when we see Mr. and Mrs. Wilcox this afternoon."

Holly Is Accused   37

"I won't mention it," promised Judy. "It's a terrible thing to be accused of something you haven't done. I know. Do you remember when I first started high school in Farringdon and everyone believed I'd stolen Lorraine's ring just because Lois had given me one exactly like it? You were the only one outside the family who believed in me. Remember when I said I wanted people to like me? I meant you, Peter, only I didn't know it. I was about Holly's age then."

"What is she? Fifteen? She looks older."

"Probably she feels older, too. She'll be sixteen next Christmas Day. That's why she was named Holly. But she doesn't like it. She feels she's been cheated out of a birthday. The Wilcox boy is about fifteen, too, isn't he?"

"Yes. His birthday's in November. His parents told me."

"They still want to see us, don't they?"

"Any time today, and we'd better get started now, as there may be some new angle for us to look into. Shall we stop somewhere along the road for lunch?" asked Peter.

"That will be nice," agreed Judy, hurrying with a few last-minute tasks.

She had just put out Blackberry and locked the door when suddenly, from around the corner of the house, Holly appeared, breathless and excited. She had taken the short cut over the hill and through the woods.

"I—I got here as soon as I could," she panted. "Judy, you and Peter must help me. Something terrible has happened. Cousin Cleo is here and she thinks I am a thief!"

"A thief!" gasped Judy. "What in the world makes her think a thing like that?"

"Because—oh, Judy! When she got home yesterday, all her beautiful antiques were missing! Not only the rose paperweight. All those shelves in the window are empty too, she says. Even the plates from the wall have been taken—"

"And the angel clock?"

"I don't know about the clock. She didn't mention it. But Judy, she accuses me!"

"Oh dear!" Judy said, turning to Peter. "We can't go off and leave Holly in a fix like this, can we?"

"Certainly not," agreed Peter. "We were just talking about what a terrible thing it is to be accused of something of which you're not guilty. The quickest way to clear yourself, of course, is to find the real thief."

"But how? I'm not used to tracking down criminals."

"No. That's our territory, isn't it, Judy?"

Judy agreed, and invited Holly to hop into the car. The trip to the Wilcox mansion would have to wait. Holly's need seemed more urgent. She was terribly upset.

"You were right about the door key, Judy," she admitted. "That wasn't a safe place to leave it. Maybe

Holly Is Accused 39

someone did see me put it back, and sneaked into the house afterwards."

"But that doesn't make sense, either," argued Judy. "Because the rose paperweight was missing before we left."

"That's so. Oh dear!" Holly sighed. "I get in deeper and deeper. Cousin Cleo is sure I carried away all her beautiful antiques in the—the forbidden chest."

"But Holly, if you open it and show her—"

"I won't! And I can't! You know that," Holly interrupted quickly.

Judy said nothing about the key she had found, although she did ask Peter to wait while she ran back to the house for something she had forgotten. Taking the key from her secret drawer, she dropped it in her change purse.

"You look as if you know something you aren't telling," Holly remarked when Judy returned to the car.

She spoke hurriedly as if she didn't expect Judy to answer. Did she know something? Judy wasn't sure. In spite of herself, she thought again of the clanking sound inside the chest. If it hadn't been breaking glass, what had it been?

"If Holly still refuses to open the chest, her cousins certainly will think she is hiding something," Judy told herself.

When they reached the Potter house Judy noticed

Holly's cousin, Fred Potter, sitting in his parked car quietly reading the morning paper. His wife, Cleo, met them on the porch. She glared at Holly, but spoke cordially to Judy and Peter.

"This whole thing has me terribly upset," she confessed. "You two have helped this family before, and I ask you, does this make sense? Holly took a chest. It was a beautiful old brass-covered chest with all the designs on it hammered out by hand. I'll admit the chest was hers to take. It's an old family heirloom, and I suppose it must have been left to Holly because of the holly wreath on the top. I don't know what is in it, but I'm sure Holly knows—"

"I don't, Cousin Cleo," denied Holly. "I haven't the vaguest idea."

"Why don't you find out?"

"Mother told me it was forbidden," Holly began.

"And so, in all this time, you've never taken a single peek inside it?"

"No," said Holly, "and I don't intend to now."

This made her cousin more furious than ever.

"Holly, you'll open that chest and show me the contents," she declared. "When I moved it to the spot where I kept it, there wasn't anything in it that rattled. Now, there is. Eric told me so."

"No!"

Judy was immediately sorry for her surprised exclamation. She caught the look of fear in Holly's eyes.

Holly Is Accused 41

"What I was about to point out," Cleo Potter continued, "is the fact that there must have been plenty of room in the chest for my glassware. Holly always liked it, too. She's told me more than once that she hoped, some day when she had a home of her own, to have a window full of antique glass just like mine. She particularly admired my blue glass hen. And there was a very valuable Millville rose paperweight—"

"Yes, the one Cousin Fred bought from my poor mother when she needed money he could just as well have loaned her," Holly interrupted.

Ignoring Holly, her cousin went on speaking exactly as if she hadn't heard the interruption.

"Holly's always had her eye on the Millville rose paperweight—"

"Just a minute," Peter stopped her. "Let's all be as reasonable as we can about this. It's a serious thing to accuse anyone unjustly."

"That's what I told Cousin Cleo," put in Holly's sister Doris, who had come out to take her part. "I said if she'd just calm down and talk this over sensibly, we might find out what really happened to her antiques."

"I know what happened to them. They were stolen!" Cleo snapped.

"Exactly," agreed Peter, "but you have no proof that Holly stole them. Judy tells me the house was left locked, but that the key was right over the door ledge where a burglar might easily find it."

"We don't have burglars in Wyville," Cleo Potter stated flatly. "It's a quiet, respectable town. In all the years I've lived there I've never had anything stolen. And now, just when Holly leaves, all my treasures go with her."

"But they didn't—" Judy started to protest, and then stopped suddenly. The rose paperweight *had* disappeared. And Judy had not gone into the dining room again before they left the house. She had not seen whether the antique glassware was still on the window shelves or not. Or whether the Majolica plates were still on the dining-room wall.

"Well, I didn't take them, Cousin Cleo," Holly said defiantly. "I took only what was mine. Didn't you see my note?"

"I saw it all right! How could I help it—tacked on the front door like that?"

"The front door!" exclaimed Judy. "But Holly left it propped up on the mantel beside the clock, the one with the lovely angels. Someone must have moved it. But who—"

"Whoever took the clock!" Cleo Potter cried. "That's gone too!"

CHAPTER VI

A Real Mystery

Much as she had admired the angel clock, Judy was relieved to hear that it too was missing. Holly was certainly not responsible for the disappearance of the clock. It had been right there on the living-room mantel still ticking away when they closed and locked the front door. Holly's cousin calmed down a little when Judy assured her of this.

"You know I'd like to trust you, Holly," she said as they all went into the house, "but it isn't easy. You've deceived me before."

Holly did look guilty, especially when she glanced toward the room she called her study. It was just back of the living room. Two doors, one on either side of the fireplace, led into it. Both doors were open. From where she was standing Judy could see the brass-covered chest with the pillows piled on it exactly as Holly had left it the evening before.

"There it is," she started to whisper to Peter.

A wail from the nursery interrupted her. Presently Ruth came out carrying the baby.

"Poor Billy!" she said. "He's still too young to understand what's being said. But he does know that when raised voices awaken him from his morning nap, it's something to cry about."

"Let me take him," Judy offered. "Maybe I can quiet him."

"If you can quiet Cousin Cleo," Ruth returned with a sigh, "the baby will be all right."

Just then Holly's uncle strode in.

"What's all the excitement about?" he demanded above the baby's screaming.

"Uncle David, please help us!" cried Doris. "Cousin Cleo is accusing Holly of *stealing!* She thinks Holly carried away a lot of valuable antiques in that chest we put under the study window."

"Humph! Is that all?" The old man seemed relieved. "Well, in that case, why doesn't she stop raising the roof and look in the chest?"

"I can't," Cousin Cleo protested. "Holly's locked it, and I don't have the key."

"Well, I don't either," Holly began, when Judy

A Real Mystery   45

quietly slipped the key she had found into her hand.

"I found this on the walk last night. See if it fits," she urged. "Once your cousin has seen the contents of the chest, she will be satisfied."

"Thanks," Holly said tonelessly. Her face was white and she stood looking at the key as if it had betrayed her.

"Well?" Cousin Cleo said. "What are you waiting for?"

"Humph! Cleo, do you really think you're going to find your everlasting glass in that child's chest?" Holly's uncle demanded. "You're making a fool of yourself!" He snorted in disgust and stalked out of the room.

A tense moment followed. Judy's heart pounded with excitement. Would she actually see the contents of the mysterious forbidden chest?

"Peter," she whispered, touching his arm.

He sensed her excitement and smiled, but he said nothing.

"Well, Holly?" Cousin Cleo demanded again.

Everybody was watching Holly. Her strange blue eyes seemed to be looking for a way of escape. Suddenly she darted into the study and closed both doors. They were usually kept open to allow light from the study windows to flood the living room. Closing them made the room oddly dark, as if a black cloud had hidden the sun.

"What's she doing in there?" Cousin Cleo said angrily after a few minutes.

Curiosity had overwhelmed Judy.

"Holly!" she called through the door. "May I come in? I'll open the chest for you if you're afraid. But there's really no reason—"

"Yes, there is," cried Holly, flinging open first one door and then the other. "The best reason in the world. The chest isn't here!"

"But it must be," insisted Judy. "I could see it from where I was standing not ten minutes ago. It couldn't just vanish—like that."

"Well, it did! It isn't anywhere. You may all come in and look for yourselves if you want to. There isn't a thing under the window where we put the chest except the cushions I piled on top of it."

It was unbelievable. They all trooped in to find that Holly was right. There wasn't a trace of the chest anywhere in the room. Judy looked behind both doors. Peter went at once to the windows. They were locked and the screens were all fastened. Judy helped him check.

"The closet," someone suggested.

But the chest was not there, either. And it could not have been removed through the windows in the short time Holly had the doors closed.

"You can't tell me Holly isn't responsible for this," her cousin charged angrily. "No burglar took the chest from under our very noses. Holly's done it herself."

"I'm a magician," said Holly with shaky defiance. "I wave my hand and make things vanish into thin air. Now you have proof of my power."

Judy couldn't keep from smiling. The charge seemed ridiculous to her, too.

"Oh, Holly! Stop making a joke of it!" cried Doris. "This is serious."

"Don't I know it!"

"Let's treat it seriously, then," Peter suggested. "It may help to look at the facts. We know, first of all, that the chest couldn't have been carried out through the living room. We were there. And yet how else could it have been removed from the house?"

"Maybe it wasn't removed."

"Well, it isn't here. That's obvious."

"It didn't drop through the floor. It *must* have been carried out. But how?"

"Through a window?"

"No, I checked the windows. There's something very queer about this," declared Peter. "I don't like it at all."

Judy pulled at his coat sleeve.

"We have an appointment this afternoon," she reminded him. "Maybe, if this Wilcox boy *is* the egg boy, and if he *did* take the rose paperweight—"

She didn't finish. Cleo Potter was shouting again,

hurling accusations at Holly. Her shrill voice carried all over the house, and Holly's uncle soon reappeared in the doorway of Holly's room.

"Now look here, Cleo Potter, I've had enough of your hollering," he said sternly, and Judy could see that he meant it. "If Holly's done anything wrong, I'll get the truth from her in private."

"In private! I want the truth now!" Cousin Cleo exclaimed.

"All I know is that the chest isn't in my room. It's gone—vanished." Holly turned appealing eyes toward her uncle. "And Cousin Cleo just won't believe I didn't hide her glassware in it."

"Well, now, I wouldn't get too upset," he returned with a chuckle. "We'll figure this thing out somehow. Just give me a little time—"

"A little time!" Cousin Cleo cried. "I've wasted a whole morning—"

"And a great many words, Cleo, but I've heard enough!" David Potter's voice was dangerously quiet. "We'll have no more of this talk—and that's final!"

"Very well, if that's the way you feel about it," Holly's cousin said in her haughtiest manner, "I shall report the theft to the police. Maybe they can find out what happened to my antiques *and* the chest!"

"That," agreed Peter, "is an excellent idea!"

Judy stared at him in disbelief. Did he realize what he was saying? Ordinarily she would have agreed with

A Real Mystery 49

him that a theft should be reported. But this was no ordinary theft. It was a mystery, and it involved Holly.

"If you do report it, Mrs. Potter," Judy pleaded, "I hope you won't make any charges—"

"I'll make plenty," Cleo Potter declared, and flounced out of the house.

A moment later Judy heard Fred Potter, who never took part in family disturbances if he could help it, starting the car.

"We must be going, too," Judy urged Peter. "The Wilcoxes expect us."

Judy had lowered her voice, but Holly heard her.

"Who are the Wilcoxes?" she whispered.

"Some people who may be able to help you out of this mess," returned Judy. "But I can't tell you anything about them yet."

"I need some help. Oh, Judy! Why did this have to happen just when I thought we were all friendly again? We did have such a nice reunion. Uncle David and my sisters have been so sweet, and it's so wonderful to have a friend like you, that I'd almost forgotten how mean Cousin Cleo used to be. I was actually beginning to like her a little—"

"Maybe you can still like her. Try and put yourself in her place," advised Judy. "She valued those antiques and they were stolen. You had been there to get your things. She's too upset to be logical."

"But I didn't take a single thing that belonged to

her," Holly protested. "You believe me, don't you, Judy?"

Impulsively, Judy assured her that she did.

"I think we can prove your innocence, too," she added, "and maybe you can help us. Peter, do you have that picture you showed me this morning?"

"It's right here in my pocket."

He showed Holly the picture. After studying it for only a moment, she said, "Why, it looks like that boy who came to the door selling eggs and banged so hard on the door. Who is it, Peter?"

"I'm beginning to think it *is* that boy who came to the door selling eggs," Peter replied as he put the picture back in his pocket.

"What does it mean?" asked Holly.

"It means we're on our way to find out who really stole your cousin Cleo's antiques," Judy called over her shoulder as she and Peter hurried back to the car.

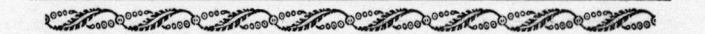

CHAPTER VII

A Nagging Doubt

"JUDY," said Peter after they had been driving a half hour or so, "have you forgotten the advice your father always used to give you?"

"What advice?" asked Judy.

For the moment she had forgotten Dr. Bolton's oft-repeated admonition: *"Use your head, Judy girl."*

When Peter reminded her of it and she began to put two and two together, she was not quite so sure of Holly's innocence as she had been when they left her.

At first Judy said nothing of her thoughts to Peter. The incident at the Potter farm had already taken up so much of their time that she knew he would have to drive fast to keep their appointment at the Wilcox mansion.

There was barely time for lunch at a roadside stand. Afterwards the car climbed steadily until they were riding along through a stretch of uninhabited woodland. Judy was strangely silent. She was thinking that the evidence was very much against Holly. Anyone less fond of her than Judy was would assume that, in order to keep Judy upstairs, Holly had produced the story for her to read. Then she had gone down and packed the glassware in the chest. Yes, and the paperweight, too. Judy couldn't forget that it had been missing and that Holly had not bothered to look for it, although she was well aware of its value. She had been in such a hurry, too. Judy couldn't help remembering how she had steered her through the front door, avoiding the dining room where the glass shelves might, even then, have been empty.

"Oh, no!" Judy's heart cried out. "She couldn't have done that."

But just the same her head went on convincing her. That clanking sound inside the forbidden chest was proof enough to satisfy her mind that some kind of glassware had been hidden in it. And then, just when the chest was about to be opened, it had vanished most mysteriously. Could Holly be responsible for its disappearance? Judy had to admit that it had vanished at a most convenient time.

"Chatterbox!" Peter teased her.

A Nagging Doubt 53

She wondered if he guessed the nagging doubt that was keeping her so quiet.

"The angel clock is the one hope," thought Judy, not realizing she had spoken her thoughts aloud.

"The angel clock?" questioned Peter.

"Oh!" said Judy, a little startled. "I didn't mean—I was just thinking—"

"So I observed. You were awfully quiet. You didn't even flare up when I called you a chatterbox."

"I'm not in the mood," Judy sighed. "Today I'm getting wrong answers to every question I ask myself."

"Try asking me the questions," Peter suggested. "Maybe I can give you some right answers."

"I doubt it," Judy said.

"Isn't it worth a try?"

Judy sighed again deeply.

"Maybe. Maybe I don't want right answers. Maybe I'd rather go on trusting Holly. I'm sure of one thing. The angel clock was stolen and Holly didn't take it, because it was right there on the mantel when we left. And if Holly didn't take the clock, isn't it reasonable to assume that she didn't take anything else?"

"It's reasonable to trust her," Peter said, "because you like her. You have a trusting nature, and I'm glad of it. Even if you trust the wrong people, it's better than being suspicious—"

"But I'm that, too," Judy interrupted him to confess.

"Holly scolded me for it. She told me I ought to be ashamed of suspecting an innocent egg boy. But if it has to be the egg boy or Holly—"

"Does it have to be either?" Peter asked gently.

"Why, no, I guess it doesn't. Maybe it's just a strange coincidence."

"But you don't think so?"

"Oh, Peter! I don't know what to think," cried Judy. "I can't keep things from you, anyway, so I may as well tell you I do have a question in my mind. Holly was so determined not to open the chest that it does look as if she had something to do with its disappearance. And there *was* something in it that rattled and clanked like glassware when we moved it."

Peter considered this gravely. Then he asked, "Would Holly have had time to pack the missing glassware in the chest while you were upstairs?"

"She may have had," Judy admitted. "I was so interested in her story that I didn't pay much attention to the time. Afterwards she hurried me out the front way. If she had taken something and didn't want me to know it—I don't believe she did, though. If it were anyone else, I might think so. But not Holly!"

"You've really taken a liking to her, haven't you?"

"Of course, Peter. She—she needs a friend."

He smiled.

"I thought that was it. When I first met you it was the other way around. You needed friends and tried

A Nagging Doubt 55

awfully hard to make people like you, especially Lois and Lorraine. They did, finally. But not until after you started being a friend—first to Irene, then to my sister Honey, and I don't know how many others."

"And every one of them has mixed me up in a mystery," Judy finished.

"You're right," agreed Peter.

"And Holly's no exception. In fact, *she* is a mystery," Judy said. "I can't figure out this uncanny ability she has to look into the past. It scares her, too. At least she says it does. But there I go, doubting her again! What kind of a friend am I?"

"A very good friend, I should think. Nobody wants blind loyalty."

"I hadn't thought of that. I'm not blind to what's happened. It's just that it doesn't make sense. That glassware I heard rattling around in the chest doesn't have to be the same glassware I admired in the window, does it? My heart tells me Holly didn't take it, and yet I can't exactly blame her cousin. What else could she think when the glassware was gone? And now the chest is gone, too, so we can't prove a thing!"

"I'm not so sure of that."

"What do you mean?" asked Judy. "Do you already know something?"

"Only something of human nature," Peter answered.

This exasperated Judy. "You're as bad as my brother Horace," she charged. "He always acts so important whenever he knows anything that it makes me want to show him how wrong he is."

"You're welcome to show me I'm wrong if you can. In fact," Peter added, "I'd rather like it."

"But how can I?" asked Judy. "I don't even know what your theory is. If you believe Holly's innocent, then I don't want to show you that you're wrong. And if you don't, why on earth did you urge her cousin to report everything to the police? Won't that get Holly in deeper than ever?"

"Not unless she's guilty," Peter replied.

"I wish I could be sure of that," sighed Judy. "You rely on facts. But sometimes facts do condemn innocent people. I rely on something else—I don't know just what it is. Anyway, I believe in Holly. I don't think that was a made-up story about the chest. Do you, Peter? I'm sure Holly really has such a strong feeling against opening it that she'd let herself be accused of something she didn't do rather than disobey her mother's last command. But there's another solution she may not have thought of. She could give someone else permission to open it."

"And you hope that someone else will be you?"

"Of course! Wouldn't it be thrilling?" exclaimed Judy. "If I opened the chest I wouldn't be disobeying anyone, would I? I'd find out what's in it and satisfy my curiosity, if nothing more. And I might clear Holly—"

A Nagging Doubt 57

"First," Peter reminded her, "you have to find the chest."

"That brings us right back where we were before," declared Judy. "We seem to be getting nowhere."

"Fortunately, the same thing isn't true of the car. So, if you want those questions of yours answered—"

"There are only three of them," she interrupted. "Where is the chest? What is in it? And why did Holly's mother forbid her to open it?"

"May I suggest a fourth question that we are now on our way to answer? Who is the egg boy?"

"But Peter, I know who he is. He's Harold Wilcox."

"Okay," said Peter as he turned the car into a private road. "This leads to the Wilcox place. Let's see if you can convince Mr. and Mrs. Wilcox that their son was seen peddling eggs in Wyville yesterday afternoon. And if so, why was he doing it? That's another question I'd like to have answered."

"So would I," agreed Judy, a new doubt assailing her as she gazed at the turreted mansion now showing itself atop the hill they were just beginning to climb. It reminded her of the Farringdon-Pett dwelling, and something of her old awe of wealth and position made her forget, for the moment, that real happiness has nothing to do with possessions.

"Oh, Peter!" she began. "That unhappy-looking egg boy couldn't have lived in a palace like this! Wouldn't you feel like a king if you lived here? I'd feel like a queen and love every minute of it. Don't you wish—"

She didn't finish.

The road up the mountain was narrow and circuitous. At that very moment another car flashed into view and met them head on. Peter hugged the bank and slowed down to make room for it to pass, but it was going at such a rate of speed that the driver lost control.

"Look out!" shouted Peter, his face suddenly white.

Judy gave a gasp of horror as the other car careened crazily and then toppled over the embankment at the lower side of the road.

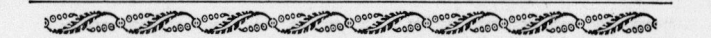

CHAPTER VIII

After the Accident

"He must have been coasting. I gave him plenty of room to pass."

"I know you did, Peter. It wasn't your fault."

In spite of Judy's reassuring words, Peter was still noticeably shaken by the accident they had just witnessed. He climbed out of the car. Judy followed, sliding under the steering wheel. The door on her side was tight against the wooded hill and could not be opened until the car was moved. Probably it had received a few scratches, but neither Judy nor Peter was thinking of that now.

"It will be a miracle if someone hasn't been killed," she said as she joined him on the road, "but maybe we can still help."

"We can try," agreed Peter, taking her trembling hand.

When they reached the embankment and peered fearfully over, they were treated to a sight that made them gasp with astonishment as well as with relief.

The car, after its leap down the mountainside, had turned completely over. With its wheels in the air, it lay in a gully at the lower side of the road. But what surprised Judy was the fact that the two men crawling out of the overturned car seemed less shaken than she was.

"They told me this make of car would take plenty of punishment," the older of the two men remarked, "but I didn't expect anything like this."

"Good thing it was your car," his younger companion commented. "Mine would have been a total wreck."

"You and I shouldn't be seen together. Bad for business," the older man said, shaking his head. "We'd better keep this accident out of the papers. This is a secluded spot. No cops around. There won't be any of the usual mob to complicate matters. It's going to take a derrick to get this thing out of here, though."

"Even then we can't be sure the motor will run."

The younger man made some further comment that Judy couldn't hear, although their voices did carry as they walked around to inspect the capsized car and comment on the extent of the damage. Evidently de-

After the Accident

ciding that nothing could be done without the help of a wrecking crew, they started off down the gully to a spot where they could reach the road without clambering up the steep bank on the lower side.

Judy and Peter hurried to meet them.

"Weren't either of you hurt?" asked Peter as the two men, puffing from exertion, reached the level of the road.

"We're both alive. Hold on a minute! Are you the driver of the other car? This is going to cost you money! We'll need help from a garage to get my car up on the road again."

With this not too friendly announcement, the older of the two men introduced himself as Stanislaus R. King, presenting an impressive business card.

Appraiser of antiques, it said.

Judy looked at the card and then at Peter. Her eyes said things.

The younger man made himself known as Jack Hauser, of New York. After introducing Judy as his wife, Peter assured the two men firmly that he would have his own insurance man investigate the circumstances of the accident, and asked courteously to see the car owner's license.

"What about shock?" Jack Hauser wanted to know, as Peter and Mr. King exchanged licenses.

"Shock!" exclaimed Judy. "We're the ones who suffered shock. We thought you'd both been killed.

There was plenty of room for you to pass if you hadn't been going so fast—"

"She's right. It was our fault," Mr. King interrupted pompously. "I can see the young lady here is something of an appraiser herself."

And he gave Judy a look that belied his white hair and dignified appearance.

"You must have been coming from the Wilcox place at the top of the hill," Peter surmised after a moment during which time he had been thinking fast.

"Would you care to ride back up with us?" asked Judy. "You can telephone a garage from there."

The younger man seemed inclined to accept this invitation, but Mr. Stanislaus R. King shook his head decisively.

"You're very kind to offer assistance," he said, "but I really must be on my way. Important business matter. There's a garage within walking distance, I'm sure. I'll stop there, and send someone out here to take care of this wreck."

"We'll drive you to the nearest garage if you wish."

Peter's offer, too, was refused.

"I can walk. Good for the constitution," declared the white-haired man. "If you want to see me in action," he added, "come to the antique show at Madison Square Garden two weeks from today. Got any antiques? Bring them along if you want to, and I'll appraise them

After the Accident 63

for you. Might as well know the real value of your treasures."

"Thank you. I may do that," replied Judy.

After one more rueful look at the wrecked car in the gully, the two men took leave of Judy and Peter and continued down the winding road to the main highway.

"I wish they had come with us. Mr. King is limping a little," Judy observed.

"The poor old man!" Peter commented absently.

Judy looked up at him in surprise.

"Aren't you sorry for him, Peter?"

"Not particularly. I'm more interested in the fact that he is white-haired, tall, and dignified—and his license plate number starts with M and ends with 0-0-2."

"It does!"

Peter nodded. "That man will stand investigation and I'd like to have the job. So he's an appraiser of antiques, eh."

"What do you suppose he was doing up at the Wilcox mansion?" Judy asked.

"Appraising antiques, no doubt."

"I'd like to see them," Judy said.

"Keep your eyes open then," Peter advised. "I intend to tell Mr. and Mrs. Wilcox all about the accident. It will explain our delay."

"I hope so. We do run into things—"

Peter chuckled ruefully.

"This bank, for instance. The car burrowed into it like a rabbit. I'll have to back out. You wait there on the road and tell me how I'm doing."

He had some difficulty starting the car. But soon it went into reverse, sending a volley of pebbles and loosened dirt in Judy's direction.

"Hey! What is this?" she cried. "Anyway, it's crawled out of its hole. Peter, it needs washing."

"What? Your face or the car?" he inquired impishly from the driver's seat.

"You would leave me out here in the way of all that debris and then make fun of me," she charged.

After repairing the damage to her face as well as she could without water, she dabbed a little powder on the tip of her nose. Then she climbed in beside Peter and they continued on their way up the mountain. They met no more cars and in a very short time reached the palatial Wilcox residence.

"Whew!" exclaimed Peter, gazing up at the turrets. "This really is a palace. It didn't seem this elegant before."

"It scares me," admitted Judy, who was seeing it for the first time. "Maybe I don't want to be rich after all."

"You've already made your choice," Peter teased her.

Judy knew what he meant. She had married him when

she could have married Arthur Farringdon-Pett and lived in a turreted mansion almost as grand as this one. But she would never regret her choice. Life with Peter was one unending adventure. The fond look she gave him told him so. But what she said was, "It would be a nice life—servants to wait on you hand and foot, and this lovely garden taken care of by someone else."

She could see a gardener in the distance clipping a hedge beyond the stretch of green lawn.

"Not a weed in it," she marveled, thinking of her own lawn dotted with dandelions.

Once she had dreamed of having a formal garden like this one at the side of the massive brick and native stone mansion. Nature had taken over in her own garden, and now there were wild daisies in it. A daisy wouldn't be tolerated here!

"It's all pretty perfect, isn't it?" asked Peter.

"Too perfect," she replied. "I like our place better."

"And I thought you were dreaming of being a princess in a palace like this! I guess I can't read your thoughts after all."

"I hope not!" exclaimed Judy. "Well, do we dare beard the lion and lioness?"

"You're forgetting," Peter reminded her, "that they're just two frightened people who have lost their boy."

This sobered Judy, although the elegance of her surroundings continued to impress her.

As Peter parked their car in the circular driveway, behind a large and shining limousine already parked there, Judy suddenly became conscious of the dust on her suit. But it was too late to give it a brushing. A butler, bowing as Judy had seen them do on the screen, was already at the door.

"Mr. and Mrs. Dobbs?" he inquired stiffly. "You are expected."

And he ushered them into the most luxurious living room Judy had ever seen.

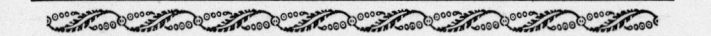

CHAPTER IX

A Possible Clue

"I don't see any antiques, do you, Peter?"

Judy whispered this, moving closer to him after the butler had departed, leaving them alone in the luxurious living room.

"Antiques?" Peter inquired, taking in the elegance of their surroundings. "I'm afraid I wouldn't recognize an antique if I met one. What about that carved piece next to the window?"

He indicated a table on which stood a modern lamp with a green dragon for a base.

"That's Chinese," Judy guessed. "The rug, of course, is oriental. Isn't it beautiful? Everything looks fairly new. Modern furnishings seem a little out of place in an old house like this, don't they? I imagine it must have been built at least a hundred years ago. People went in for turreted mansions then."

"They're too expensive to keep up now—"

Peter stopped abruptly as a heavy footstep sounded on the broad stairway leading down into the living room. Presently a stout, baldish gentleman appeared and extended his hand.

"How do you do, Mr. Dobbs!" he boomed in a voice that startled Judy. "I'm sorry to have kept you waiting. Matter of fact, we'd about given you up. Figured you realized your mistake and decided not to bother us with any more details about this egg peddler. But I see you're a persistent pair. So this is your wife? The young lady who thinks she saw *my* boy peddling eggs!"

"It was no mistake, I can assure you," declared Peter. "Her friend also identified your boy as the egg peddler they saw in Wyville."

"But that's ridiculous!" Mr. Wilcox protested. "My boy has been kidnaped, I tell you. He was seen getting into a car with a stranger at three o'clock yesterday afternoon. Your job is to find that car."

"I think we've already found it, Mr. Wilcox."

After answering a few questions that Mr. Wilcox fired at him, Peter asked his permission to call the local police. He made a report of the accident.

After being assured that no one was hurt, Mr. Wilcox breathed easier.

A Possible Clue

"Well, I'm glad of that! So it was Stanislaus R. King's car my boy got into! That gives the whole thing a different complexion," he declared. "Yes, sir! An entirely different complexion!"

"In other words, Mr. King is a friend of yours?" prompted Peter.

"Exactly! Known him for years. Admired him, too! Lives in New York, but has a country place not far from here. He's president of our Collector's Club."

"What sort of a club is that?"

"Group of men who collect things. Anything from stamps to butterflies."

Judy noticed that Mr. Wilcox had a habit of chopping off the beginning of his sentences, especially when he was excited.

"So you collect things!" she thought suspiciously. "No doubt your son does, too. Things that belong to other people, such as that rose paperweight."

She wanted to convince herself of this, so that she could still trust Holly. But she said nothing. Peter knew what questions to ask.

"We get together once a month to talk about our hobbies," Mr. Wilcox continued in answer to Peter's next question. "In fact, the next get-together was to have been here."

"Indeed!" said Peter. "Was that the reason for Mr. King's visit?"

"Partially."

"You called off the meeting, I suppose?"

"No," he said shortly. "A man can't let family matters upset other people's plans. The members of the club are anxious to see my collection."

"And what do you collect, Mr. Wilcox?"

"I'll show you. If you'll just come upstairs—"

He broke off as a florid-faced woman of generous build appeared at the head of the stairs. Her eyes were red-rimmed as if she had been crying. Suddenly it seemed odd to Judy that Mr. Wilcox was no longer very much concerned about the missing boy. Apparently Mrs. Wilcox did not feel the same way.

"Can't you show off your possessions another time, Henry?" she pleaded, hurrying down the stairs. "They've come about Harold. Is there any news of our boy?"

Before Peter could answer, Mr. Wilcox boomed, "Good news! That kidnaper was a figment of your imagination, Mabel. Actually, the car Harold was seen getting into belonged to our good friend, Stanislaus R. King. Or so Mr. Dobbs tells me. No doubt Mr. King wanted to accommodate us, and gave our boy a lift to wherever he was going—"

"But where was that? And what happened to him afterwards?" cried Mrs. Wilcox despairingly.

"We'll question Mr. King," Peter promised. "That's the next thing to do. Is this other man, Jack Hauser, a friend of yours also?"

A Possible Clue

"Jack Hauser?" they both questioned.

Apparently the name did not register.

"Yes, he was with Mr. King."

And Peter told Mrs. Wilcox about the accident, assuring her that nobody had been hurt, although it did look, at first, as if someone would certainly be killed.

Judy remained silent, but her mind was working fast. *"You and I shouldn't be seen together. Bad for business,"* Mr. King had said to Jack Hauser—if that really was the man's name. He had hesitated before giving it, almost as if he were making it up. What business were they talking about? Judy couldn't help wondering. And now it turned out that Mr. King had been alone when he visited the Wilcox mansion. Had Jack Hauser appeared out of nowhere on the way down the mountain? He couldn't have been coming from another house, as this was a private road.

"I suppose he could have been a chauffeur," Mrs. Wilcox ventured. "But what does it matter? Finding Harold is the thing. If he wasn't kidnaped, why didn't he come home for dinner or later last night?"

Peter suggested the possibility that he might have run away.

"This may be his idea of an adventure," Peter said.

"But why? Harold has everything!" cried his mother.

"What about a chance to work and earn a little spending money for himself?" inquired Peter.

"Why should he work?" Mr. Wilcox demanded.

"His allowance is more than generous. He could come and go as he pleased and do what he liked with his money. Besides," Mr. Wilcox concluded, "the boy has no ambition."

"My husband is right about that," put in Mrs. Wilcox with a sigh. "Harold wouldn't even pick up after himself. The upstairs maid is constantly complaining about it. She says there's no reason why a boy his age should make all that work for others. Of course, she doesn't scold him to his face. I wouldn't allow it."

"But it sure is more peaceful around here today," said Mr. Wilcox.

Judy and Peter exchanged glances. Right there was a possible clue to the boy's disappearance.

"Perhaps Harold foresaw that," Peter said.

Mr. Wilcox turned on him angrily.

"Do you mean to imply that my boy *preferred* the life of an egg peddler? Why, that's preposterous!"

"Is it? You worked when you were a boy, didn't you, Mr. Wilcox?"

"Naturally," he retorted. "I was ambitious. I wasn't going to see my children raised in poverty as I was. I worked my way up. I had to. But I've started my boy at the top."

"If you don't believe we've been good to him, come upstairs and see for yourselves," Mrs. Wilcox invited. "Why, there wasn't a thing that Harold wanted that

A Possible Clue 73

we didn't give him. Come with me and I'll show you his apartment."

"His apartment?" questioned Judy. "Most boys consider themselves lucky if they have a room to themselves."

"That's what I keep telling Harold," his mother agreed. "We've given him the entire third floor. Besides his bedroom, he has his own private bath, a hobby room, a TV room and a little balcony overlooking the garden. He can bring his friends up there whenever he likes."

"Does he bring them?"

Mrs. Wilcox sighed and shook her head.

"No. That's something about Harold that I can't understand. He prefers to visit them. Naturally, none of his friends has the luxuries he has."

"Perhaps," Peter said, "you can add to this list of his friends you gave me yesterday. I've checked with every one on the list and they all tell me the same story. They haven't seen Harold since Mr. King drove up in front of the school and offered him a ride. We'll check with Mr. King, of course. But there may be a boy we've missed."

"I'm sure there must be. He never introduces his friends to us. But perhaps we can find his address book in one of his coat pockets. Are you coming up?" Mrs. Wilcox asked.

"You go, Judy," Peter said a little wearily. "I've already seen Harold's apartment. The maid helped me check to see if any of his clothes were missing besides what he was wearing."

"And were there?"

"Not that we could discover. She wasn't very familiar with his clothing and Mrs. Wilcox was too upset last night to go through them with us. Suppose you help her. Mr. Wilcox and I have something to discuss down here."

"Ready?"

Mrs. Wilcox reminded Judy of a well-fed pigeon poised for flight.

"They think they love him," thought Judy, "but they don't either of them really know their son." And a sick feeling went through her that two people could value possessions so much and a boy so little.

Aloud she said politely, "Yes, Mrs. Wilcox, I'm ready."

CHAPTER X

A Valuable Collection

Judy was curious about the rest of the rooms in the great turreted mansion, and followed Mrs. Wilcox eagerly. Her feet, on the carpeted stair treads, made almost no sound. It was like walking on cushions. When they reached the first landing, everything, from the dark wainscoted walls to the polished stair rail, shone suddenly with a soft rosy glow.

Presently a stained-glass window came into view. It shed its light over a domed alcove at the turn of the stairs.

"This must be the inside of one of the turrets!" exclaimed Judy. "It's beautiful. It's like coming into church. And this—"

She stopped, speechless.

In a glass-topped case below the window she saw something that quite took her breath away.

"Wait a minute, please!" she called out breathlessly to Mrs. Wilcox. "Here's something that I want to see!"

"Oh!" said Mrs. Wilcox, turning abruptly. "I do beg your pardon. That's the collection Mr. Wilcox intended to show you."

Judy was tremendously excited.

"But you didn't—he didn't say it was a collection of old glass paperweights. Maybe now we really can find Harold!"

Mrs. Wilcox looked at Judy questioningly.

"I don't see how this collection of paperweights can help."

"Wasn't Harold interested in it?"

"Not a bit," his mother replied. "My husband is the collector of the family. I doubt if Harold ever looked at the collection."

"Didn't he ever stop on his way upstairs to admire it? I should think a boy would—"

"Harold wasn't like other boys." Judy noticed that his mother used the word *wasn't* as if she had already accepted the fact that her boy would not return. "He was—well, there wasn't anything that really interested him."

"Did you tell my husband that?"

She nodded.

A Valuable Collection

"I believe Mr. Wilcox mentioned it in answer to one of his questions. Harold has never done very well in school or in sports. As we already told you, he has no ambition."

Although not a pious girl, Judy was tempted to quote the Bible as her brother Horace sometimes did. "*Judge not, that ye be not judged* . . ." She still had the feeling she was in church because of the stained-glass window. Would a boy feel that way too? Judy didn't know.

"This doesn't make sense," she thought as she gazed into the case where more than a dozen exquisite paperweights in many shapes and sizes had been arranged with the utmost care. Who had arranged them? Mr. Wilcox, probably. He wouldn't have let Harold touch his precious collection. And how would the boy feel about that? Would he have hated it? Or would he have felt something of the spell Judy was feeling now?

Mrs. Wilcox waited a little impatiently while Judy's gray eyes searched the collection. The missing rose paperweight was not there. She did find a pansy weight nearly as delicate and beautiful as the one Holly had shown her, and another that looked as if pieces of candy were swirling about inside the round glass ball.

"Here's one with an eagle in it!" she exclaimed as Mrs. Wilcox returned to stand beside her. "Where did your husband find all these beautiful paperweights, Mrs. Wilcox?"

"The eagle one belonged to his great-grandfather. It

was given to him after he came home wounded from the war."

"That was the Civil War, I suppose?"

"Yes, the weight was made at Millville when the finest work was being done there. See the flag clutched in the eagle's claws?"

"I see it," said Judy. "The stars in the blue field almost shine, and how real the feathers on that eagle look!"

"His eye is the finest ruby glass. That weight is very valuable," declared Mrs. Wilcox. "It started Mr. Wilcox on his collection. Mr. King appraised the collection at ten thousand dollars and said it would be worth considerably more if Mr. Wilcox could get hold of a Millville Rose to complete it."

"A Millville Rose!" exclaimed Judy. "But I know—"

She stopped herself in time. Peter had told her that when she was working with him it was better to get information than to give it.

"You don't know where he could buy one, do you? I mean a really good one," Mrs. Wilcox prompted her.

"No," said Judy, "I'm afraid I don't. I've never seen but one Millville rose paperweight and it's—it's not for sale."

"Are you certain of that? My husband would pay almost any price—"

A Valuable Collection

"Did Harold know that?" Judy interrupted to ask.

"He may have heard his father speak of it. I don't know. As I told you before, the collection didn't interest him. If Harold ever had a hobby, it was electric trains. Would you care to see them?"

Judy said she would, although her thoughts were still on the paperweight collection. Was it true that Harold had no interest in it? What would go on in the mind of a boy who had everything handed to him on a silver platter? That is, everything except love and approval. Would he be happy? Judy doubted it.

When Mrs. Wilcox showed her Harold's hobby room, as she called it, Judy noticed at once how dusty his trains were. It was a beautiful layout, though. In all, there were three sets of trains with tracks, switches, lights, tunnels, bridges, and tiny villages. There was even a lake with a mirror for water and tiny swans reflected in it. Mrs. Wilcox sighed discouragingly as Judy exclaimed over it.

"I thought it rather nice myself," she admitted, "but you can see how dusty it is. I'll have to speak to the upstairs maid. I'm afraid Harold soon lost what little enthusiasm he had for his trains."

"Did his father set them up for him?" asked Judy.

"Mercy, no!" exclaimed Mrs. Wilcox as if such a thing were quite unheard of.

"He didn't do it himself, did he?"

"No. He couldn't. He's had them since he was six.

At first he did enjoy them," his mother admitted, "but before we knew it, he was trying to take them apart. That wouldn't do, of course. They're quite expensive. They were purchased with all the equipment, just as you see them. I had an electrician come in to install them as, naturally, Mr. Wilcox wouldn't be interested in a toy."

"Poor little boy!" sighed Judy. "Even his trains were so expensive that he couldn't play with them!"

The sigh was to herself. Mrs. Wilcox closed the door to the hobby room and said, "This is his bath with glass-enclosed shower."

"It's really luxurious, isn't it?"

Judy was tempted to add, "Too luxurious," but restrained herself as it was more important for her to learn exactly what was in this woman's mind. Straightening a lavender towel on its rack, Mrs. Wilcox turned and walked through the boy's bedroom until she came to a large closet.

"Well," she said as she opened the door, "I suppose we may as well go through Harold's clothes."

One by one, she took the hangers from the closet, noted this or that article of clothing, searched the pockets if there were any, and handed the hanger back to Judy, who replaced it on the bar.

Finally Mrs. Wilcox came to an old, soiled leather jacket.

"He liked this," she began. "He wouldn't wear any-

A Valuable Collection 81

thing else. It was all I could do to make him shed it when warm weather came. It's like having him here just to hold it . . ."

Suddenly Judy became aware of the fact that Mrs. Wilcox was crying over the old jacket. Judy looked at Harold's mother compassionately. But even in that moment she felt less sympathy in her heart for Harold's parents than she felt for the boy himself.

"And that's bad," she thought. "Very bad!"

For, in order to prove Holly's innocence, she had hoped to find Harold guilty. What his mother had told her about his lack of interest in the paperweight collection was hard to believe. Judy wondered what Peter would think. Anyway, she had some facts for him.

"I could get more," she was thinking, when Mrs. Wilcox spoke to her.

"Let's go down," she said. "The atmosphere up here is depressing. I think I'll have these rooms completely done over if Harold doesn't come back."

CHAPTER XI

A Disrupted Plan

JUDY agreed with Mrs. Wilcox that the atmosphere in Harold's room was depressing. And it was no less so downstairs where the butler had just bowed himself in to announce that tea was being served in the drawing room . . .

"Why is a drawing room called a drawing room?" Judy wondered later, when she and Peter were in the car again.

"It's an abbreviation of *with*drawing room," he explained in answer to her question, "and was I ever glad to withdraw from it!"

"Me, too!" agreed Judy. "I thought they'd keep us there sipping tea and eating sandwiches forever!"

A Disrupted Plan

"We did accomplish one thing, though," Peter acknowledged. "We finally convinced them that Harold might be happier doing something useful, like selling eggs."

"But do they *care* about his happiness?" cried Judy. "Oh, I know they think they do! Mrs. Wilcox cried when she found his old leather jacket in the closet. For a minute I felt so sorry for her, and then she spoiled it all by announcing that she'd have the room redecorated if Harold didn't come back. Wasn't that an outrageous thing to say, Peter?"

Peter agreed. He had convinced the Wilcoxes that it probably wasn't a kidnaping after all, and they had agreed to turn the whole matter over to the local police.

"They don't know it—" Peter was speaking of the Wilcoxes again—"but they supplied just about all the information we need. Now we go into action."

"But Peter," Judy protested, "you told them it was not an FBI matter."

"Officially, it isn't—if their friend, Mr. Stanislaus R. King, is as innocent as he wants to appear to be."

"Poor Harold," sighed Judy. "They didn't say one affectionate thing about him. The poor boy must have felt their disappointment in him. If he did run away, it seems almost a shame to bring him back."

Peter agreed. "But if you want to get back the rose paperweight," he added, "you'll have to find the boy who took it. After seeing his father's collection I'm convinced that Harold knew its value and that he carried something besides eggs in that covered basket."

"Oh dear!" Judy said, not sure whether to be glad or sorry Peter had reached the same conclusion she had.

Peter slowed down the car as they rounded the blind curve that had caused the accident on the way coming up.

The brakes squeaked as he brought the car to an abrupt stop when they had reached the foot of the hill. A tow car was just pulling Mr. King's battered car out of the ditch. A small crowd had gathered to watch. But there was no sign of either Mr. King or his companion, Jack Hauser.

"Know why?" asked Peter when Judy commented on their absence.

She shook her head.

"No, tell me."

"Well, I can't be sure," Peter admitted, "but if the sheriff I talked to on the telephone has anything to say about it, they're down at his office explaining a few things, including the little matter of picking up Harold Wilcox in front of the school yesterday."

Judy sighed.

"So it is an FBI case after all?"

"If it's a kidnaping, which I very much doubt. But there's a lot we don't know."

"Let's find out then," Judy suggested.

A Disrupted Plan   85

"That," declared Peter, "is exactly what I intend to do. We're on our way to the sheriff's office now."

Judy felt a sudden rush of elation, but it was short-lived. At the sheriff's office it was learned that Mr. King had given a satisfactory account of what had happened the previous afternoon.

"He recognized the boy as the son of his friend, Mr. Wilcox," the sheriff explained, "and offered him a ride. He said he intended to take him all the way home, but Harold asked to be let off at the five-and-ten-cent store."

"Did you check with the store?" Peter wanted to know.

"Haven't yet, but I'm sending a man over now," the sheriff assured him.

"Do that," Peter agreed, "and I'll call back later for his report."

Outside the sheriff's office, Peter turned to Judy and said seriously, "With the money that boy could get for the rose paperweight, he could have taken off for far places by this time. It's going to be hard to trace him."

"But would he sell the paperweight?" asked Judy. "He knew his father wanted it."

"Obviously," Peter said, "he didn't bring it home."

Judy had to think that one out. If he had brought it home, she reasoned, the pieces of the puzzle would have fitted without too much blame falling on the boy, Harold Wilcox. Somehow, Judy felt she had to be loyal to him as well as Holly—probably because his predicament filled her with sympathy. After all, she told herself, a boy couldn't be blamed for trying to win his father's approval. Or could he? Helping himself to the rose paperweight, even if he had wanted it for his father's collection, would still be stealing. Maybe he did it on impulse and thought better of it. Or maybe he didn't do it at all!

On the other hand, if Holly had taken any of the antiques, she would certainly have taken the rose paperweight. She might even have considered it rightfully hers, since it had once belonged to her mother.

"Maybe she did," Judy said suddenly. "That would explain it."

"Did what?" asked Peter, giving her a puzzled glance.

"Oh dear!" Judy chided herself. "I'm thinking in circles again, but I didn't mean to think out loud. Peter, what do we do next?"

"I have a plan of action," he replied, "and you can help me if it isn't too late. Some of them may be closed, of course, but there's a list of antique shops in the classified telephone directory—"

"And I'm to call them and ask if anyone has brought in a rose paperweight since four o'clock yesterday afternoon?" Judy anticipated.

"Exactly," Peter agreed, "and while you're doing it, I'll report to Mr. Trent on the day's activities."

A Disrupted Plan

Mr. Trent was Peter's immediate superior and the one from whom he usually received his assignments. Judy had been quite impressed by him when she first met him. But that was before she knew that Peter would one day be an FBI agent himself.

"He's twice as clever as Mr. Trent, and just as handsome," she thought fondly as they parted to disappear into different telephone booths. Judy took the classified telephone directory and started calling right down the list.

The Antique Mart was closed. So was the Art Shop. But an old lady in the Attic Shop answered to say no, she'd never seen a Millville rose paperweight, though she'd read that they were valuable.

"I'm afraid I couldn't buy one even if 'twas offered to me," she finished. "That is, unless I had a buyer. A gentleman did ask me to get him one, years ago when the shop was doing better. Wilcox was his name. He lived in Scranton, seems to me."

Judy thanked her, as soon as she could get in a word, and hung up. So Mr. Wilcox had lived in Scranton. Probably he had bought the mansion on the hill when real estate values were down.

"A place like that wouldn't be easy to sell," she reflected. "Even the Farringdon-Petts would have a hard time finding a buyer for their place."

She called the next number on her list. Brandt's Department Store. They had an antique department and this was one of the evenings they kept open. The voice that came over the wire sounded familiar.

"Lois!" exclaimed Judy. And suddenly all their shared experiences came back with a rush. The friendship ring, their high school burning as they stood and watched, the summer together in the Thousand Islands . . .

"Don't tell anyone I'm working here," Lois Farringdon-Pett was saying. "I love it, of course, but the family does have to keep up appearances."

"Don't you wish it didn't?"

"Yes, but that's a secret. Oh, Judy!" Lois exclaimed warmly, "I'm glad you know. Now what can I do for you?"

"Just tell me if you have a Millville Rose—"

"A Millville Rose!" exclaimed Lois. "Have you just come into a fortune?"

"No, a mystery," laughed Judy. "It's information I want."

"Well, if I hear of one I'll certainly let you know," Lois promised. "Wouldn't it be thrilling if I could help you solve a mystery again?"

"It certainly would," declared Judy.

After promising Lois that she would tell her about it when she saw her, Judy hung up and called the next number on her list. Most of the shops were closed by now. Judy copied down the numbers of those that did not answer, intending to telephone them in the morning.

A Disrupted Plan

Last on the list was the Wyville Antique Shop. So far none of the shops, except one called the Hearth, reported having a rose paperweight, and that one, from the description given her, was not the paperweight Judy sought.

"Oh dear!" she said to herself, dialing the Wyville Antique Shop, "I guess this finishes them. Hello! Yes, I'm calling to ask . . . What's the matter? *Hello!*"

A woman with a pleasant voice had taken down the receiver and said, very politely, "Wyville Antique Shop. May I help you?" And then, before Judy could finish her sentence, something had happened.

"What is it?" cried Judy.

A strangled gasp was her only answer. Then she heard a crash and the connection was broken. It sounded as if the telephone had been deliberately put back on its hook.

CHAPTER XII

A Strange Coincidence

"Peter," Judy began excitedly, "something's hap—"

She didn't finish because, by a strange coincidence, they were saying the same thing.

Judy had rushed from the telephone booth to find Peter impatient to be off. And now he was saying, "Judy, something's happened! There's been another robbery."

"But how did you know?" she asked in bewilderment. "It happened only a minute ago. I'm sure it was something terrible, if not a robbery, then something worse. I'll tell you about it on the way there. It happened in the Wyville Antique Shop."

It took Peter a moment to grasp what she was saying.

"But that isn't the robbery I was talking about," he

objected as they hurried toward the car. "This one was reported by a woman who lives in the outskirts of Wyville. Someone entered her house through a window and picked a number of family heirlooms from among her possessions. She wasn't sure they had anything more than sentimental value. At first she wasn't going to report it, but when she found the window had been forced open—"

"Maybe someone forced their way into the Wyville Antique Shop, too. Maybe my telephone call interrupted a robbery! I thought the woman fainted. But someone put the telephone back on the hook."

"That does look suspicious. We'll find out who it was," declared Peter. "It begins to look as if Wyville isn't the quiet, respectable town Cleo Potter believes it to be, doesn't it?"

"Yes," agreed Judy, "and it begins to look as if we might clear Holly of suspicion without ever opening her precious forbidden chest."

"What about your curiosity? Doesn't it still have to be satisfied?"

"Not necessarily. I can't find out everything, anyway," Judy replied hurriedly as she slid into the seat beside Peter and he started the car.

"Right now," she continued, "I'm more interested in finding out what happened at the Wyville Antique Shop and what we can do to help that poor woman who answered the phone."

While he drove toward Wyville as fast as he dared, Judy told him exactly how it had happened while Peter, in turn, told her how he had learned of the second robbery.

"I called the sheriff to get his man's report on whether Harold had been seen—"

"In the five-and-ten-cent store?" inquired Judy.

"Yes, and he was—but not until about quarter to five. He bought a cheap suitcase, a shirt, and a couple of pairs of socks. But the time is wrong. It didn't take Mr. King almost two hours to drive him from school to the store. We want to know what happened during those two hours."

"Naturally. Mr. King will have an explanation, of course."

"He'd better have," Peter said fiercely. "We're going to question him again as soon as we locate him. I don't trust King. If I'd been in the sheriff's shoes I wouldn't have permitted him to leave Wyville in such a hurry. But on this other thing, as I was telling you, I called the sheriff right after he'd talked to the woman who says she was robbed. Her name is Mrs. Vaughn and she lives on Elm Street, not far from Oak—"

"And the Potters live at Number 12 Oak—"

"Exactly," agreed Peter. "And from the address you gave me, this antique shop seems to be in the same end of the town."

"I wish Dad were here," Judy said. "I'm not sure

A Strange Coincidence 93

that was a robbery, but whatever it was, that poor woman may need a doctor—"

"Well, here we are, we'll help her. It didn't take long, did it?" asked Peter as he stopped the car before an attractive little shop on Cherry Street, just around the corner from Main.

As they opened the door of the shop a bell tinkled, but no one appeared in answer to it.

"That's strange," Peter commented. "I guess you're right, Judy. Something *is* wrong. It doesn't look as if the shop has been robbed, though."

"No, it doesn't," she agreed, giving the display of antiques a hurried glance, "but where's the woman?"

"We'll have to find her. *Hello, there!*" Peter shouted.

An echo was his only answer. It sounded ghostly, as if the china figurines in the tall cabinet at his side had answered. A clock chimed, as if startled by the call. Judy shivered and moved closer to Peter.

"I don't like this," she whispered. "Don't call again, Peter. Wherever she is, she can't answer. Let's look for the telephone."

There seemed to be nothing so modern as a telephone in sight. Even the electric light switch, if there was one, had been placed in some obscure spot where neither Judy nor Peter could find it. An old kerosene wall lamp with a polished brass reflector lighted the dim interior of the shop.

"It makes shadows!" exclaimed Judy. "Isn't it

spooky in here, Peter? If I didn't know that poor woman must be somewhere hurt or dying, this would be quite an adventure."

"But not your first—in an antique shop," he reminded her.

Judy knew he was thinking of one of the most thrilling mysteries she had ever solved—THE INVISIBLE CHIMES. Ever since then, antique shops had held a certain fascination for her, and this shop was no exception. It contained everything from the tiny figurines she had noticed to a massive cigar store Indian who glared down at her so suddenly that she jumped.

"How!" Peter said solemnly.

"If I ever want to scare anybody to death," Judy announced, "I'll buy one of those things and keep it in a dark corner."

In another corner she noticed a screen and peeped behind it to find a washbasin with a towel rack and a holder for paper cups on the wall behind it.

"Something modern at last," she thought.

Meantime Peter, searching in a different part of the shop, had discovered a door. Judy hurried toward him just as he opened it.

"There's the telephone!" she cried, darting through the door ahead of him and almost stumbling over the inert form on the floor. Quickly she bent and found the woman's pulse.

"She's still alive. But we'll need help."

A Strange Coincidence 95

"There's a drugstore just down the street."

"Then go, Peter! They'll know of a doctor near by. I'll be all right," Judy assured him.

A doctor's daughter, Judy knew what to do in an emergency. The woman's face was pale and her breathing shallow. Fearing she might be suffering from shock, Judy quickly covered her with a warm patchwork quilt displayed near by. Then she loosened her clothing and said gently, "Is that better?"

There was no response. Judy began applying cold cloths to the woman's head. The water she had discovered came in handy.

"This ought to bring you to," Judy thought as she worked over the woman.

She was in her middle fifties, Judy judged, and would be pretty except for her ghastly pallor. Her eyes were closed. Not a flicker of an eyelid repaid Judy for her ministrations. Again she checked her pulse, finding the same faint flutter she had first detected.

"Please wake up!" she begged, but to no avail.

The shop door opened and Peter came in with another man. As Judy called out to them, a faint sigh came from the woman's lips.

"You're coming to! Can you hear me?" asked Judy, bending over her again.

"Yes—I hear." She passed her hand across her forehead as if in pain and then tried to raise herself.

"Not so quickly, please," Judy cautioned her. "It

is better for you to lie flat until a doctor examines you. I'm afraid you are quite ill—"

"Ill? Oh!" The woman suddenly struggled to sit up, and faced Judy. "Who—who are you?"

"I'm the girl who was calling you when—when this happened," Judy explained. "I've brought help."

The woman turned her head to see who had entered the shop.

Judy introduced herself and Peter.

"Thank you. You've been very kind," the woman said. Her voice was stronger now. "I'm Mrs. Ott and that's Mr. Berger, the druggist, with your husband."

Refusing assistance from Judy, Mrs. Ott got rather unsteadily to her feet.

"Well," she said, trying without much success to regain her ordinary tone and manner, "is there anything I can do for you before I close the shop?"

"But we came to help you," Peter protested.

"You'd better let me get Dr. Page over to examine you—" the druggist began.

"I don't need a doctor," Mrs. Ott interrupted, "and if I did, I wouldn't call that young greenhorn, Dr. Page. I'd call Dr. Bolton of Farringdon."

"He's my father!" exclaimed Judy. "If you really want him, I can get him here fast."

Mrs. Ott sat down rather heavily in one of her own antique chairs and looked Judy straight in the face.

"You're telling me the truth," she said, as if there

had been some doubt in her mind before. "You're Judy Bolton, the little redheaded girl I remember in pigtails and a green-checked dress. I remember you from before the flood when your father had his office in Roulsville. I was a sick woman then. But your father discovered the trouble and I haven't had a doctor since."

"An occasional check-up is a good thing, even when you're well," Judy ventured. "I'll be glad to call my father if you want me to."

"Better let the young lady call, Mrs. Ott," the druggist advised her. "After all, you were unconscious when these young people found you—"

"Of course I was unconscious! You would be, too, if someone crept up behind you and hit you on the head," Mrs. Ott declared. She gave the shelves of her antique shop a searching glance and added vehemently, "No, I don't need a doctor. Some of my most valuable pieces of old glassware are gone! What I need is the police!"

CHAPTER XIII

Stranger Still

Not until Peter showed his credentials would Mrs. Ott say another word. After that she allowed him to report the robbery to the local authorities, and in a very few minutes the shop was filled with policemen.

"Another robbery? Somebody must want antiques awful bad," one of them said.

Judy could see he had no taste for them himself.

After a long report had been filled out, poor Mrs. Ott was utterly exhausted. She looked ready to faint again. But she was determined not to submit to an examination by Dr. Page or any other young doctor. So, finally, Judy called her father.

"I know it's late, Dad," she told him over the telephone, "but there's been a robbery and you know the victim. It's a Mrs. Ott, who says she used to be a patient of yours when you had your office in Roulsville before the flood. Someone hit her on the head and knocked her unconscious, but she won't let the young doctor in this town examine her. No, she didn't see who hit her. Apparently the robber, or robbers, crept up behind her and aimed the blow so skillfully that she immediately lost consciousness. She says she's all right now, but I think you ought to see her. She says you're her favorite doctor."

This pleased her father, Judy knew, although he merely growled in response to it. However, after some more coaxing on Judy's part, he did promise to come.

"Is Horace there?" Judy asked on impulse. "Bring him along if he is. This seems to be the third robbery in Wyville within the last week. There's a front page story for his paper if he wants it . . ."

Horace was there, very much there, in short order. And so were half a dozen other reporters. It was a full evening. In fact, the excitement lasted far into the night.

"This is really a good break, Sis," Horace kept saying.

After it was all over, Judy realized she should have asked Peter before inviting her brother to spread the news of the robbery all over the front page of the *Farringdon Daily Herald*.

"But the police would have given him the story anyway," she reasoned.

It did not occur to Judy that the robbery might have anything to do with the kidnaping of Harold Wilcox—if it was a kidnaping—until the following morning when the telephone awoke her out of a sound sleep.

"Hello!" she said drowsily into the instrument. She had let it ring for several minutes, hoping Peter would answer it. But then it had dawned upon her that Peter was not in the house.

"Oh, it's you, Horace!" Judy's voice was impatient. "I guess you and Peter never sleep! He's off somewhere. No, I don't know where and wouldn't tell you if I did. It's only nine o'clock in the morning and I didn't get to sleep last night until three. After all, I don't want bags under my eyes. Investigate *what?* I know you'd like to know who hit Mrs. Ott over the head, and so would everybody else. Do you have to have a follow-up on the robbery story? Oh, all right. I'll be ready. Good-bye!"

Judy was thoroughly awake now. She searched through her bureau for her candy-striped blouse, pulled it over her head, and zipped up the skirt of her blue suit.

Blackberry, who had helped his mistress solve more than one mystery, gazed at her solemnly out of his great green eyes.

"You win," she told him. "I'll let you yowl just once at the cat in the mirror and then we'll go down to breakfast. It's cereal for both of us."

Stranger Still   101

When Judy reached the kitchen she found that Peter had already made coffee and opened a can of peaches. She also found a little left-over salmon in the refrigerator to flavor Blackberry's cereal. Then she spied Peter's note.

"In the refrigerator, of all places!" she exclaimed as she opened it.

The note said:

> *Dear Angel:*
>
> *You looked so peaceful sleeping that I decided not to disturb you. Have a good breakfast and take it easy today. I'm working with the police. A stolen car has been found near Olean, New York. This may be the getaway car used by the robbers. Transporting stolen goods over a state line is a Federal offense which makes this my case. Wish me luck and get a good rest.*
>
> *Love,*
> *Peter*

"Rest!" Judy exclaimed. "With that brother of mine—"

A rap on the front door interrupted her.

"Ready, Sis?" Horace inquired when Judy unlocked the door to let him in.

"If you can call a dusty house, unwashed dishes, and chickens that haven't been fed, ready—" Judy began. But Horace was already busy helping her.

When Judy returned from the chicken house where she had left the hens a generous portion of their special brand of mash, she found every dish washed and the kitchen spick and span.

In another ten minutes the whole house was in apple pie order and Horace's cream-colored convertible was on its way.

"I have just one little question to ask you," Judy said as they turned onto the main highway. "Where are we going?"

"East," Horace said.

"Silly!" Judy scolded. "That's obvious. Wyville is east of here. Are we going to Wyville?"

"That's where the robbery was, isn't it?"

Judy didn't answer him. She could see that her brother was in one of his uncommunicative moods. That meant he was thinking. As Judy had plenty of problems to think through herself, they drove for half an hour in silence. They had left Farringdon and the convertible was climbing up the first long hill beyond the town when Horace spoke suddenly.

"Peter tells me Holly may be involved in this," he said.

Judy was annoyed.

"Well, she isn't. Not in this," she said. "These two robberies are the work of professionals. Peter will tell you that."

"He did. He stopped by on his way to wherever he was going—"

"Did he tell you about the forbidden chest?"

"Yes, he did tell me a little. It was a funny thing how it vanished, wasn't it? That house is a tricky place, though. Maybe it fell through a trapdoor."

"No, the floor is solid."

As they talked about it, all Judy's curiosity returned. Could the disappearance of the forbidden chest have been a robbery, too? Horace thought so.

"I could feature it as a mystery—"

"And make still more trouble for Holly? I wouldn't do that if I were you," Judy advised.

"Was the chest an antique?"

"Yes, but I don't know what was in it. If we can prove Cleo Potter's stolen glassware wasn't in it—"

"I get it," Horace interrupted. "All I can say is that if any more robberies break out near Roulsville or Farringdon, you'd better watch those antiques Grandma left you."

"But Horace, they aren't really valuable—"

"That's what Mrs. Vaughn thought about her antiques. She wasn't going to report the robbery at all until she found that window forced open. There may be others who were robbed and didn't report it."

"Wouldn't it be exciting if we could find them? Is that what you're planning, Horace?"

"I don't know how we'd go about it," he admitted. "My plan is to call on the people who've been robbed. I told Peter about it and he suggested taking you along just in case some egg boy might be involved. He warned me not to wake you too early, but I didn't think nine o'clock was early and if this news is to be in the afternoon paper, we want something the morning papers haven't scooped."

"You'll get something," Judy prophesied, "but it won't involve the egg boy if I can help it."

"What about Holly?"

"It won't involve her, either."

"That's what I wanted to be sure of," Horace said. "I've taken a liking to that little girl. What's more, I trust her."

"So do I," declared Judy, and this time she meant it. "As for the egg boy—"

"Guilty as heck, from what Peter told me!"

"Oh, Horace, don't judge him so harshly," Judy chided her brother.

"How else can I judge him?" he asked. "It was Peter himself who told me a Millville rose paperweight was missing from the Potter house in Wyville right after the egg boy left, and that Holly got the blame for taking it."

"Yes, but there's still a possibility it wasn't missing until after the robbery. I may have overlooked it."

"You? Sis, you don't overlook anything!"

"Thanks," Judy said, "if that's a compliment. It's true, I couldn't find the paperweight. Holly didn't look. She was suddenly in a terrific hurry and so we left and then—well, it must have been very soon afterwards that the house was robbed. You can see why Holly was blamed. But now, with all these other robberies taking place, it ought to be easy to prove her innocence—"

"And the egg boy's guilt," Horace finished for her.

"If that's what you're trying to prove, I'm not sure I want any part in it," declared Judy.

Horace glanced at her quizzically.

"Just what do you know about this egg boy?" he asked.

"Not nearly as much as I'd like to know," Judy replied guardedly.

Surely Peter hadn't told Horace there was a possibility that the egg boy might be the missing Harold Wilcox. So far, none of the newspapers had been informed of the boy's disappearance.

"Obviously," Horace said, "you know something you're not telling."

"I do know this much," Judy retorted. "Peter said last night that the antique shop robbery looked like the work of an organized gang, and when he expresses an opinion like that, it's usually based on facts. I wish—"

"I know," Horace interrupted. "You wish he'd taken you with him. But don't worry, we'll find out plenty. You haven't met Mrs. Vaughn, have you?"

Judy's gray eyes suddenly shone with anticipation. Peter had planned this because, for some reason, he had not been permitted to take her with him.

"No," she answered, "but I'm certainly looking forward to it. What's she like?"

"You'll find out," Horace promised. "You know, it's been the same in all three robberies," he went on thoughtfully, "always some rare old glass was taken that only an expert could have spotted. Strange, isn't it?"

"Very strange," agreed Judy.

But she was thinking of the forbidden chest and how it had vanished almost before her eyes. That had been the strangest thing of all.

CHAPTER XIV

More than Coincidence

JUDY was silent for a little while, thinking.

"To tell you the truth," she confessed presently, "I'm almost afraid of what we may find out."

"Why?" asked Horace. "Because of your friend, the egg boy?"

"He isn't my friend," denied Judy. "I only saw him once, or rather his reflection. It—it's just because he's so young and he had such a defeated look about him. I don't want to be the one to—to trap him."

"If he is the thief, you certainly don't want him to get away with it, do you?"

"Oh, Horace! I don't mean that," cried Judy. "Of course I don't. Criminals don't ever get away with it, anyway. They have to live with themselves whether or not they're caught. A criminal wouldn't be a pleasant person to live with."

"You mean his conscience would hurt him? They get hardened after a while."

"But then they can't enjoy things, either! I mean the way we do. This river, for instance." They were just crossing the Susquehanna. "Horace, do you think it sparkles and shines in the sunlight for them the way it does for us?"

"I doubt it. Golly, do you see that castle up there?"

He stopped the car to point out the Wilcox mansion and Judy tried to pretend that she was thrilled with the sight. Actually, seeing it again made her sick at heart.

"What have I done?" she asked herself. "I've set Horace on the trail of this story and, eventually, the whole thing will come out in the papers."

Judy could imagine the headlines:

WILCOX BOY, FEARED KIDNAPED, STAGES
SERIES OF ROBBERIES

"But he can't be alone in this. Oh dear!" thought Judy. "Why can't I stop feeling sorry for him?"

Aloud she said, "Come on, Horace. I thought you were in such a hurry to get a follow-up on this robbery story. We can't gaze at castles for the rest of the day."

"You're right," sighed Horace as they drove off. "They aren't very practical."

"I should think not! Me, I'm satisfied with a remodeled farmhouse in Dry Brook Hollow. But maybe you can build a palace on the land Grandma left you. I mean when you find your princess," Judy added teasingly.

"That'll take time. Honey's going to be a career girl, she tells me. She's completely wrapped up in her art work. Can't see anything but the fabrics she's designing—"

"You mean anything but the fabrics and the young man who manufactures them," Judy amended. "Mr. Dean has turned over most of his business to his handsome son, Forrest—"

"Must you bring that up? Well, I'll have to wait for Holly to grow up, I guess."

"Holly!" exclaimed Judy. "That won't solve your problems. She's going to be a career girl, too. Didn't I tell you about the story she's writing? It actually comes to her out of the past, as if she'd lived before."

"Now you are teasing," declared Horace.

"No, I'm serious," Judy assured him. "I was lost in her story when the egg boy came to the door. Otherwise I might have paid more attention to what was going on downstairs. Horace, you may not believe it, but Holly has created a character, Felicity, who seems so real you actually expect her to step out of the pages and talk to you. Holly thinks she *was* real, but has no idea how she knows about her. It just comes to her, she says. Sometimes her sudden—what would you call them?"

"Revelations?" Horace suggested.

"Maybe. Well, she says they frighten her. Anyway, my dear brother, I wouldn't recommend Holly if you object to a career girl. Who knows? Maybe some day she will be a famous novelist."

"And Honey will be a famous artist and will probably marry Forrest Dean to boot. Oh, me!" sighed Horace. "The future is horrible to contemplate."

"Don't worry. We'll dig up somebody for you," Judy promised. "Here we are in Wyville."

They were just entering the business section of the town. Beyond it was the better residential area where the streets were named for different kinds of trees.

Horace turned off Main Street on Cherry, stopping at the Wyville Antique Shop to find out if there were any new developments.

There were. A young man who introduced himself as Mrs. Ott's son-in-law, and looked as if he would be able to handle half a dozen robbers single-handed, said he had a clue.

"There's been a boy hanging around here lately, my wife's mother says. She buys eggs of him," he related, not noticing the look of dismay that crossed Judy's face. "He always insists on walking through the shop instead of going around to the side entrance like most

More than Coincidence 111

delivery boys. What's more, he asks a million questions on the way."

"What sort of questions?" asked Horace.

Judy was keeping silent, trying to organize her thoughts.

"About the antiques, how old they are, where they were made and all such things," he replied. "Now it doesn't seem natural to my mother-in-law that such a young boy would be interested in antiques for their own sake. His questions show that he's no dummy. That boy knows values."

"Did he give his name?"

"Just his first name," was the reply. "He said to call him Joe. He has dark hair that keeps falling down over his forehead, and big dark eyes. I don't know where he lives, but the eggs he sells are from Clover Farm."

"Thank you," said Horace, flashing Judy a triumphant grin. "Now we really have something to work on."

He would have dashed out of the shop immediately but Judy kept him a little longer while she asked after Mrs. Ott's health.

"She's feeling fine," her son-in-law declared. "In fact, she'd be working today if your father hadn't advised her to rest. Dr. Bolton is your father, isn't he?"

Judy nodded, stalling for time to think. She still couldn't understand why Peter, of all people, wanted publicity. It was she who had set Horace on the trail of this news, to be sure, but Peter had gone right along with her.

"I thought I recognized you as the famous Judy Bolton. You've solved quite a few mysteries, haven't you? Your brother is reporting all this for the *Farringdon Daily Herald*, I suppose."

"If I'm not too late," Horace said.

"You were asking about my mother-in-law," the young man went on. "I started to tell you that Dr. Bolton advised X-rays. In fact, she's up at the hospital now, having a thorough check-up."

"By *young* doctors?" asked Judy, giggling.

He laughed.

"Your father advised it."

"Anyway, tell her we were asking for her," Judy said as they left.

In the car again, Horace said excitedly, "That's a clue that is a clue! Now I'm certain that your egg boy is involved in this chain of robberies."

"Yes, I'm afraid he is," Judy admitted. "Just the same, *I* don't think he could have robbed a strong, healthy woman like Mrs. Ott all by himself. And he couldn't be cruel enough to knock her over the head and then loot the shop with her lying there. He—he's only a kid, Horace. Maybe he did have some part in the robbery. But there must have been others, too. Real criminals who influenced him. Let's see what Mrs. Vaughn has to say."

More than Coincidence

"What will she know about it?" asked Horace. "She was away when her house was robbed, and had no idea—"

"Just a minute," Judy broke in. "You want headlines for your paper, don't you? You want to approach this story from a new angle so you'll be able to scoop the morning papers? Well, wouldn't it be a strange coincidence *if all the people who were robbed were on the same egg route?*"

"That would be more than coincidence," Horace declared. "That would be *news!* We'd spread it all over the paper."

"Oh dear! That's just what I was afraid of," Judy said.

Horace gave her a searching look.

"I can't figure you out, Sis," he admitted. "It's hard to tell if you're with me or against me."

"I'm with you, Horace. Neither of us wants to hurt anybody, and I know you'll be fair. But it's important to get your story straight before it's printed. I want to clear Holly, naturally, but not if it means putting the blame on some other innocent person."

"You're referring to the egg boy, I take it."

"*If* he's innocent. As I mentioned before, let's see what Mrs. Vaughn has to say."

CHAPTER XV

Horace's Headlines

Five minutes later Judy and Horace were standing on the brick steps of Mrs. Vaughn's neat blue and white Colonial home on Elm Street. The entire front lawn was shaded by one of the great elms from which the street had probably taken its name.

"Isn't it peaceful here? Maybe I would prefer a place like this to a castle after all," Horace commented as he pushed the bell.

Like all the other trimmings on the door, the bell was brightly polished.

"A sign that Mrs. Vaughn must be a better housekeeper than I am," thought Judy ruefully.

In answer to the bell the door was opened by a stately, gray-haired woman who smiled coldly and said, "I'm sorry, but if you're selling anything—"

Horace's Headlines 115

"We're from the *Farringdon Daily Herald*," Horace interrupted, including Judy in the introduction. After all, his editor had once told her she could work for him any time.

Judy flashed her brother a grateful smile as he went on to explain that a new clue had been discovered through which it was hoped the robber, or robbers, might be apprehended.

"You can help us, Mrs. Vaughn, if you will," Judy added.

"Of course, if it means recovering my stolen antiques. Won't you step inside?" she invited more hospitably.

Once inside the charming living room, now bare of the precious keepsakes that had given it a true Colonial atmosphere, Mrs. Vaughn launched into a full account of the robbery. Judy and Horace listened sympathetically, if a little impatiently. They had already heard most of the details that were being supplied by their hostess.

"But perhaps you already have this information," she finished.

"Some of it. Now may I ask you a question?" Judy inquired.

"Certainly," responded Mrs. Vaughn. "I'll be glad to answer any queries you have."

"It may seem unrelated to the robbery, but do you buy eggs of Clover Farm?"

"Of course." She seemed surprised. "Everyone in this neighborhood does. They're fresh and you can buy them cheaper than you can in the stores. Besides, it saves shopping time. A boy delivers them to the door."

"Will you describe the boy, please?"

Mrs. Vaughn described Harold Wilcox, even to his defeated expression and his characteristic habit of throwing back his head to toss a lock of unruly black hair out of his eyes.

It was just as Judy had feared.

"If it has to be Holly or the egg boy," she had said to Peter. And he had asked gently, "Does it have to be either?"

She had hoped, up until now, that it wouldn't have to be. But what she had just learned changed everything. Harold's mother was wrong. Antiques did interest the boy, but not in a way that would bring him closer to his father. They interested him only, Judy feared, for what he could get out of them. He wasn't peddling eggs because he wanted to do something useful, as she had hoped. He was peddling them as an excuse to gain entrance to homes or shops where antiques or art treasures were on display. Then . . . But what did he do then? Did he actually return to steal the antiques? More likely, he was a member of a gang of young hoodlums. His parents had known so little of his friends or where he spent his time.

"Did you ever ask this egg boy into your home, Mrs.

Horace's Headlines 117

Vaughn?" asked Horace when he saw that Judy had finished questioning her.

"Once," she admitted. "I was baking cookies. He was such a young boy, not more than fourteen or fifteen. I thought he would like a cookie—"

"So he waited in the living room while you went into the kitchen to bring him one," Judy anticipated.

"Why—yes."

"I'm afraid he didn't want a cookie nearly so much as he wanted a chance to—well, to evaluate the antiques you had in your living room," Judy said. "I'm sorry about it. I wish it could have been an older boy, one I didn't pity so much."

Mrs. Vaughn sighed. She seemed really distressed to hear how she had been tricked. "I liked the boy, too. He seemed so unhappy. I thought perhaps his family might be in need . . ."

"Far from it," thought Judy.

"I'm afraid I tipped him rather generously," Mrs. Vaughn continued. "You see, he's new on the route. I believe he's substituting for Al Kunkel, the boy who delivered eggs before."

"Thanks. That helps," said Horace, jotting down the name.

"You say he's new? Just how long has he been delivering eggs?" asked Judy.

"About a month. A friend of mine, Mrs. Blessing, was on his route, too, and so was a Mrs. Dwight on

Maple Street. They weren't robbed exactly. But right after he'd been to their houses, they both missed a couple of pieces—Wedgwood, I think."

"Wedgwood!" exclaimed Judy.

She was thinking of the antiques her grandmother had left her, and hoping the robberies would not break out in the vicinity of Roulsville or Farringdon. That is, if they hadn't already. She still couldn't understand the disappearance of the forbidden chest unless someone had lifted it through the window so expertly that even Peter couldn't tell how it was done. In that case, her own antiques were certainly in danger. Her mother, in Farringdon, had a few precious Wedgwood pieces, too.

"Were they large pieces?" Horace asked.

He was taking notes of everything in his familiar little black book.

"Not too large," Mrs. Vaughn replied. "He could have concealed them in his basket. I told you he was selling eggs, didn't I? He delivers them fresh from Clover Farm."

"Our next stop," declared Judy.

But Horace shook his head. Apparently, he had something else in mind.

"Thank you, Mrs. Vaughn," he told her hurriedly. "Come on, Judy!"

"But Horace," she protested, "don't you think we ought to check all this at Clover Farm?"

"There isn't time," he replied. "If this news is to get in this afternoon's paper I've got to be quick about it."

Judy was dubious about the wisdom of printing everything they had learned, but she couldn't tell Horace why.

"Whoever runs the place won't like it if you mention Clover Farm without checking there first," she protested.

"Okay, I won't mention it. They'll get it later. But you promised me headlines and now I've got them. MYSTERY BOY SOUGHT IN WYVILLE ROBBERIES."

"Mystery boy," Judy repeated. "That sounds corny. Why don't you wait and find out who he really is?"

"I'll save that for tomorrow's paper," Horace threw back at her as he ran for the nearest telephone.

In less time than seemed possible the *Daily Herald*, carrying the story, was on the stands. Horace's headlines were almost as he had described them to Judy.

MYSTERY BOY SUSPECTED IN CHAIN ROBBERIES
By Horace Bolton

Wyville—An egg peddler known only as Joe to his customers is linked to three, and possibly five, robberies in which antiques and art treasures valued into the thousands were stolen.

Home-owners and shopkeepers throughout this and near-by counties are warned to keep watch of their valuables until the boy is apprehended. About five feet, four inches in height, with straight black hair and brown eyes, he is being sought by the police . . .

"And by us," Judy put down the paper to add. "That is, if your headlines don't scare him away."

"They may make him run home to his mother—"

"And to the shelter of his castle," thought Judy.

"Don't look at me with those daggers in your eyes," begged Horace. "I'm only quoting Peter. That was the general idea, I took it. The boy must be a runaway. Obviously, he didn't give his right name at Clover Farm."

After Horace had telephoned in his news they had checked with the dairy people and learned very little. The egg boys were in business for themselves in the same way that newspaper boys are. Each had his own route, paid wholesale prices for the eggs he delivered, and sold the eggs for only a fair profit. The name the boy had given to the people at the farm had been Joe West, and the address, like the name, had turned out to be fictitious.

"We have another name, though," Horace said thoughtfully as he stirred more sugar into his coffee. He and Judy had realized, at last, that they were hungry and had stopped off in a restaurant near the station.

"Of course," agreed Judy. "It's the name of the

other egg boy, Al Kunkel. That's probably his real name, too, as they told us at the farm that the parents of the regular boys were required to post a bond for them. They really were careless about their substitute boys."

"Careless! I'd say they were downright negligent," declared Horace. "There are laws about the employment of children. They didn't ask for working papers or proof of his age or anything."

"This other boy had them, though. Look!" exclaimed Judy, who had finished her lunch and was now leafing through the pages of the Wyville telephone directory. "Here's a Benjamin Kunkel. He could be Al's father. It's a different address than the one given us at the farm, but they could have moved."

"Right!" agreed Horace, gulping his coffee. "I'll call them."

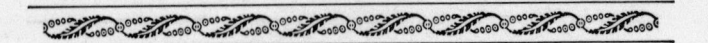

CHAPTER XVI

An Underground Adventure

Horace's telephone call was completed in a very short time. He returned to the table where Judy was sitting, with a triumphant gleam in his eyes.

"You were right, Sis," he said. "Benjamin Kunkel is Al's father. They don't know any kid called Joe West, but that doesn't mean much since it wasn't his real name anyway. All they knew was that one of Al's friends was substituting for him on his egg route."

"What about Al?" asked Judy. "Did you talk with him?"

"No, but I intend to. His father said he was off with his gang. They have a clubhouse in the woods and he spends a lot of time there. Sometimes he even spends the night—"

An Underground Adventure 123

"So that's it!"

Judy instantly regretted the exclamation. Horace was sure now that there was something she wasn't telling him.

"What does that spell to you?" he inquired, giving her a knowing look. "Go ahead, tell me! What are you holding back?"

"Nothing that I'm free to tell you," replied Judy. "However, I do think this clubhouse might make a good hideout for a runaway boy, don't you?"

"For a thief, you mean, and for his loot! I'm not going to let any teen-age gangster play on my sympathy," announced Horace. "I'm in favor of taking the police with us unless you know where to locate Peter."

"I don't think that's necessary."

"You never know. Mrs. Ott wasn't treated very gently," Horace reminded her.

Judy couldn't deny the truth of that statement.

"Do you know where to find this clubhouse?" she asked.

"Al's father directed me to it," her brother answered. "Naturally, he had no idea it might be a gang hideout."

"Don't jump to conclusions, Horace! You may be right, of course," Judy admitted. "Anyway, I'll call Peter. Possibly he's home by now. If he isn't I'll try and locate him through the field office. I suppose if they don't know where he is we'll have to ask the police to help us."

Horace agreed. When Judy was unable to locate Peter they left the restaurant and started for the police station after being directed there by a surprised young man who looked at them as if they might be criminals about to give themselves up.

"We're going to feel awfully foolish asking for police protection if this turns out to be nothing more than a boys' club," Judy ventured.

"We'd feel worse if they were armed and we weren't," Horace returned grimly.

"I suppose so. If only Peter were here to advise us! I'm beginning to understand why he has to carry that awful revolver. Just the same, this boy may be as innocent as we are. If he is, I hope we won't get him into any trouble. Oh dear!" Judy finished. "Here we are!"

They had come to a halt before a forbidding-looking building that they both recognized as the police station. For just a moment Judy hesitated, a little shiver of apprehension running down her spine.

"Don't worry," Horace reassured her. "We won't make trouble for anyone if we can help it."

If Judy was reassured, it was only for a moment. As they opened the heavy doors and walked into the big, bare room, a uniformed officer looked up from behind a massive desk. Judy thought he had the coldest blue eyes she had ever seen.

"You want to make a charge against this Al Kunkel?"

An Underground Adventure 125

he inquired after he had taken down the name and address.

"No," Judy said hastily. "As far as we know he has done nothing wrong."

"Then what are you bothering me for?" the officer demanded.

Horace explained the situation as accurately as he could.

"We don't want to frighten the boys," he finished. "We just want the place searched in case they've taken the loot from these robberies there. They may know nothing about them. As my sister already told you, we have nothing against this boy, Al Kunkel. It's not a criminal offense to build a clubhouse in the woods."

"Depends on whose property it's on and whether or not the lumber was stolen," the officer snapped.

Judy and Horace exchanged glances. It was too late now, but they were both wishing they had not asked for police help, especially if the boys turned out to be innocent of any part in the robberies.

"What we want," Horace stated after he had answered several more questions, "is to locate a boy who calls himself Joe West."

"Joe West!" The name apparently rang a bell. The officer reached for the afternoon paper, scanned the first paragraph of Horace's story, and said, "Well, that's different! Why didn't you say so in the first place? Think you can identify him?"

"I can," Judy spoke up. "I saw him examining one of Mrs. Potter's antiques the day she was robbed. I'm not sure, but he may have carried it away in his egg basket and returned later with his gang to rob the house."

"Mrs. Potter suspects her own cousin, according to the story she gave us," the officer said.

So this was the officer who had heard, and undoubtedly would investigate, Cleo Potter's accusation of Holly. Judy knew she would have to act fast to clear her friend.

"That was before these other robberies took place," she explained. "My brother and I interviewed the people who were robbed, and we're convinced this egg boy can tell us something. That is, if we can find him."

"Okay, let's go!"

The chief officer called to a younger man who was introduced as Patrolman Ryan. He and another policeman named Higgins were instructed to follow Judy and Horace to the boys' clubhouse. The cream-colored convertible led the way. Horace, at the wheel, followed the directions he had received over the telephone. The police car was close behind.

"We'd better go first," Patrolman Higgins advised when the two cars had pulled over to a bank not far from the path that was supposed to lead through the woods to the clubhouse.

The two policemen were friendly and talkative. They

seemed to enjoy following the path over fallen trees and through beds of wintergreen as much as Judy and Horace did. But the path seemed to lead nowhere. Before long they had passed through the little strip of woods and were out in a cleared field.

"We must have missed it, somehow," Horace said. "Mr. Kunkel was very definite about the location. It's supposed to be along this path before you come out of the woods. I didn't see any clubhouse, though."

"Maybe it's just a few sticks thrown together," Patrolman Ryan suggested. "Boys will call anything a clubhouse."

"There's a boy!" exclaimed Judy. "I mean, there *was* a boy. He disappeared back there behind that patch of chokecherry bushes."

"I saw him. He's led us to his clubhouse all right. You two keep back. We'll find it," volunteered Patrolman Higgins.

The two officers reentered the woods a little ahead of Judy and Horace. They stopped just beyond the chokecherry bushes, peered this way and that, and then looked at each other as if they were completely at a loss to understand what had become of the boy.

"Horace, they do look baffled," said Judy with a giggle.

Curious, they came nearer to see what was puzzling the two officers.

"Someone's been digging here," one of them observed from behind the clump of bushes, "but I don't see any building."

"No," agreed the other. "There's not so much as a stick."

"Look! Here's a hole. You don't think that boy could have crawled into it, do you?"

The question was not addressed to Judy, but she answered it.

"I do. It's big enough."

Patrolman Ryan bent and measured the opening with his stick. Then he shook his head.

"Maybe, for a boy. But it's not big enough for me."

Patrolman Higgins was a little larger than his companion. Even Horace had put on a few pounds lately. But not Judy!

"I'd like to try it," she volunteered. "I'm sure there's no danger. That boy we saw wasn't more than ten years old."

"Wait. We'll get the gang out of there first. Maybe then you can go in." And Ryan called out in his loudest voice, "This is the law! Come out of there with your hands in the air!"

Judy heard a terrified "Gosh, we'd better!" and presently a small, dirty-faced boy appeared. He was trying his best to crawl out of the hole and keep his hands up at the same time. And it wasn't easy!

The first boy was followed by another, equally dirty. Then another and another. Finally six trembling boys, all slim, but of assorted heights, stood before the astonished company. It was fully a minute before anyone spoke.

"Is that all of you?" the policemen asked at last.

One of the smaller boys gulped a "Yes."

Patrolman Ryan then turned to Judy.

"See anyone you know in this lineup?" he inquired.

"No," she replied after studying their faces, "but I wouldn't know Al Kunkel—"

"That's me," a thin blonde boy spoke up, "but I haven't done anything wrong."

"I believe you," said Judy. She could see the boy was frightened, and spoke reassuringly. "The police aren't looking for you, Al. They're looking for a friend of yours who calls himself Joe West. He's the substitute on your egg route."

"Not any more he ain't. I'm taking it back," Al said. "I don't want any trouble with my customers."

"Trouble? Sonny, you've got real trouble if we find any stolen goods in that hole you just crawled out of," Patrolman Higgins declared in a voice that was suddenly hard.

"May I look now?" asked Judy. "I have a flashlight."

"Might as well," the policeman agreed.

"Better tie this around your head to protect your hair," Horace added, lending Judy a clean handkerchief.

One of the boys offered his coat for added protection. He even seemed a little eager to show off the underground hideout and, after being searched by the cautious Higgins, volunteered to go first and show Judy around.

"This is the way you do it," he explained, and dived head first into the hole.

Judy followed him cautiously. What would she find in this dark underground hideout?

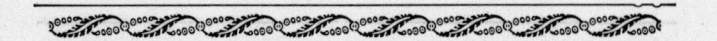

CHAPTER XVII

A Dangerous Risk

"SEE? There's nothing here except our games and stuff. It's like Al told you. We weren't doing anything wrong."

The boy who had preceded Judy into the underground clubhouse was standing up now. To her surprise, Judy was able to stand up, too. As she did so, something brushed against her face. She shivered and then laughed. It had been nothing but a dangling root from one of the bushes which were now over her head.

"It is creepy in here," the boy admitted. "But we like it."

Judy could understand that. Creepy places had a certain fascination for her, too. She flashed her light around until it fell on an improvised table. Apparently the boys had been having a quiet game of monopoly by candlelight.

"But what an odd place to play! Aren't you afraid the roof will fall in on you?" Judy asked.

"It can't," was the reply. "The roots and branches overhead hold it up. Besides, we covered the place where we did the digging with good strong planks. They make a nice ceiling."

"I can see that. Did you boys dig out this cave all by yourselves?"

"Most of it. A tree that fell over in a storm gave us the idea. The roots are our back wall."

Judy's young informer seemed proud of the job he and his friends had done, and well he might be. What she had thought might be a hideout was nothing but a playhouse—a secret playhouse. Then Judy spied an opening to another underground room and peeped inside.

"This looks as if somebody had slept here!" she exclaimed, noticing an old mattress covered with a patchwork quilt. Not an antique, she hoped! There were no ornaments here except such treasures as any boy might bring to his clubhouse. An oriole's nest hung from an orange crate. Inside, on a shelf, was a textbook entitled "Planet Earth," and a stack of school papers. The name on them was Alfred Kunkel.

"Al studies here," the boy informed her when he saw she was leafing through the schoolbooks. "I'm Skid

Keller. We're all members of a secret club. Sometimes Al sleeps here, but my mom won't let me. Only the big boys do."

"What big boys besides Al?" Judy asked curiously.

"Oh, Bud Strober and Hank Larsen, and for the last couple of nights, a new boy called Hal. I don't know his last name."

"You don't think Hal could be short for Harold, do you?"

"Maybe. We don't call each other by sissy names."

"Is Hal about my height, with brown eyes and straight black hair that keeps falling over his forehead?"

Skid looked at Judy in surprise.

"Sure, that's Hal. Do you know him?"

"No, but I know his folks. They're looking all over for him. When was he here, Skid? When did you last see him?"

" 'Bout half an hour ago," the boy replied. "Maybe not that long. He left just before you and the cops came."

"He did? Do you think he saw the cops?"

"No, but he thought they were after him. It was on account of something in the paper," Skid explained. "One of the kids came in with it. Hal took a look and then, all of a sudden, he says, 'Got to be going, kids! See you in jail if the police catch up with me.' We thought he was joking, and then he grabbed his suitcase—"

"His suitcase?"

"Yes, he had brought a lot of stuff here."

"What sort of stuff, Skid?"

"Books, clothes, games, stuff like that. He always has plenty of money. He gave Al ten dollars for his egg route. But what's the matter? Don't you want to see the rest of the clubhouse?"

"Not now," Judy said. "It's a lovely clubhouse, but I'm like Hal. I've got to be going. How do we get out?"

"This way."

Skid pushed against something that looked like the underside of an old cellar door, and a wide opening appeared. This time Judy did not have to wriggle through like a ground mole. She stepped directly out into the chokecherry patch. The door had been well concealed behind the bushes.

"We leave this door open most of the time so we can get air. It's secret," Skid added in a whisper.

A blue-uniformed coat appeared before them.

"It *was* secret, you mean. Sorry, Skid," Judy apologized. "It isn't now."

"Come here, Ryan," Patrolman Higgins called to his companion. "There's a big door hidden back here in the bushes. We'd better search this hideout."

"First," Judy advised, "you'd better talk with this boy. He's given me some important information."

"He has?" Patrolman Higgins seemed surprised. "We couldn't get a thing out of the rest of them."

A Dangerous Risk

"You will tell the policeman what you just told me, won't you, Skid?"

The boy's lip began to quiver.

"They'll put me out of the club. I didn't like Hal much, but Al Kunkel did."

"The egg boy," Judy explained. "He was a member. Thanks, Skid, for your coat and for—for everything you told me. Officer, please be nice to him. I'm sure these boys are all innocent. My brother and I will be going now."

"That's all right," the policeman told her. "You just leave everything to us."

"We will. Thanks a lot." And Judy hurried back to where Horace was standing amid the group of frightened boys.

"Save your questions till later. We're getting out of here *fast*," she told him as they ran back along the path to where the convertible was parked next to the police car.

"What's up?" asked Horace. "Things were just beginning to happen. I wanted to see that hideout myself."

"There was nothing much to see except a bed where the egg boy spent the last two nights. It gave me an idea. When's the next bus or train out of here? He left not more than half an hour ago and if we hurry we may overtake him."

"We'll hurry then. Did you find anything else?"

"Nothing stolen, if that's what you mean. Right now I'm more interested in finding the boy. Let the police search the place and question those boys if they want to. I doubt if they'll learn much. I didn't—"

"You must have learned something pretty important," Horace interrupted.

"Only where the egg boy's been sleeping. He left in a hurry when he saw your newspaper story, but I don't think he went home."

They had been hurrying back to the car. Now Horace climbed behind the wheel and inquired, "Which way do you think he'd go?"

"Where would this road take him?" asked Judy.

Horace withdrew a map from the glove compartment and studied it briefly.

"The way we came, it goes back to Wyville, of course. But if he followed it in the other direction it would take him to Binghamton and the main line of the Lackawanna—"

"Good! We'll follow it that way, then. He may try to hitchhike to the railroad."

Horace leaned low over the wheel, his eyes fastened upon the winding road ahead while Judy kept a sharp lookout to the right and left.

"Oh dear! I don't see anyone walking," she announced after the first few miles had been passed. "Maybe he did go back to Wyville after all. A bus goes through there at eight o'clock and it's after seven now."

"Shall we try it?" asked Horace. "I think we can

A Dangerous Risk 137

make it back to the bus station. That bus goes right through Farringdon and Roulsville. You can board it and have a talk with the boy if you think it will do any good. I don't mind driving home alone."

"That is a good idea," agreed Judy. "There's a garage driveway. Can you turn here?"

"I think so. There's not much traffic."

Horace had just turned into the driveway, giving Judy a clear view of the road ahead. They were coming to an intersection where several cars had halted, waiting for the traffic lights to change.

"There's a boy!" Judy suddenly exclaimed. "He's walking at the side of the road and he looks as if he's carrying a suitcase. Don't turn, Horace! He may be the boy we're after."

Since they were driving and the boy was on foot it seemed to Judy that it ought to be a simple matter to catch up with him. But she had not counted on the fact that the boy was hitchhiking.

"We're gaining on him," she exulted. "He looks like the egg boy. Oh dear! Someone's offering him a ride!"

"We'll keep that car in sight," Horace promised. "It's a blue Plymouth. I can't see the license plates, but it's heading toward the railroad."

"We guessed right then! Horace, if he takes the train I'm going to follow him."

"How far?" asked her brother. "It takes money to ride on trains."

"I've got some money."

"How much?" he inquired.

Judy opened her purse and counted every bill that was there.

"Thirty-eight dollars and a little change. I guess it wouldn't take me *very* far," she admitted.

Horace just grinned. He was keeping the blue Plymouth in sight without much difficulty. Presently they overtook a big truck and both cars were obliged to crawl along behind it. The driver of the blue car tooted his horn.

"He's trying to pass that truck on the hill. If we stay behind it we're sure to lose him!" mourned Judy.

"Don't worry," Horace told her cheerfully. "This crate was built for speed. If he can pass the truck, so can I."

"Please don't try it!" begged Judy "We can probably locate the boy again at the railroad station. Anyway, I'd rather lose him than my life. Oh, Horace! Watch out!"

As the blue car swung to the left to pass the truck, a huge moving van loomed up over the hill ahead. The driver of the Plymouth, seeing his danger, swerved back in line. Horace jammed on his brakes, but not in time. The convertible met the back of the car ahead with a terrific jolt.

"Judy!" cried Horace as his sister slumped down in the seat beside him. "Sis, I'm sorry. I stopped as fast as I could. Are you really hurt?"

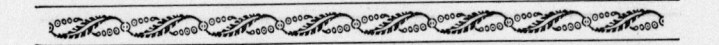

CHAPTER XVIII

Judy's Plan

"I'M ALL right, Horace!" Judy was half laughing and half crying from her awkward position on the floor of the car beside him. "I'm not hurt, except for a scraped elbow. I just didn't want him to see me. He turned around."

"Who did? The egg boy?"

"Yes, when we bumped, but I'm sure I slipped out of sight in time. He probably thinks you're alone. I'm surprised they didn't stop to see if there was any damage."

"I'm still keeping them in sight. There would have been plenty of damage," Horace declared grimly, "if this car weren't equipped with extra-strong bumpers. The Plymouth is okay too, from the looks of it. That truck has picked up speed going downhill and we probably won't have to pass it after all."

"That's good! I don't like passing big trucks on uneven roads. I'm not anxious to get very close to that Plymouth, either. My disappearing act may not work a second time."

"Why was it necessary?" asked Horace. "You told me this egg boy had never seen you."

"That's true," asserted Judy, "but if I should have to follow him by bus or by train I don't want him to see me until he's well on his way to wherever he's going. By then I'll just be another passenger—"

"I get it," said Horace. "I guess it was worth a good scare and a scraped elbow. But how about Peter? He doesn't know of this—this plan."

"You'll have to tell him about it, Horace," Judy said. "I'll be off for parts unknown. But Peter will understand."

"I hope so," sighed Horace, increasing his speed in order to keep the other car in sight.

They had left the Susquehanna Valley far behind and were now driving through dense and lonely woods with only an occasional farmhouse to be seen. So intent was Judy upon watching the car ahead that she paid little attention to the scenery, although here in the mountains it was really beautiful.

"He's driving fast," Judy observed uneasily. "We're coming into a town, I think. I see lights ahead. If we're not careful we'll lose him at this next intersection. My plan won't be worth much if we do."

"Your life won't be worth much if I drive any faster. Blast!" ejaculated Horace as he jammed on the brakes. "He made the light and I didn't, but we'll overtake him yet!"

As soon as the light changed Horace made up for lost time. The convertible fairly roared along the highway, but traffic was heavier now, and it had grown dark. To her dismay, Judy could no longer see the car they had been following.

"Don't worry! We'll win this race yet," Horace announced ten minutes later. "This city we are now entering is Binghamton, and here comes the train!"

Little by little Horace gained on the speeding train until they were racing even. The highway ran parallel with the tracks for some distance. Fortunately, they were not obliged to cross.

"We made it! The train is slowing down and here we are at the station!" Judy cried out joyfully.

As Horace brought the car to a halt, Judy noticed a blue car just driving away from the well-lighted parking area across from the depot.

"I was right! He did bring him here. Now I'm sure it's the egg boy. There he goes into one of the coaches!" Judy exclaimed as she jumped out and dashed in pursuit of the disappearing boy.

"Wait a minute!" called Horace, running after her.

"You may be going on a long trip. Here, take this."

He pressed a folded bill into her hand. Judy accepted it without looking at it and climbed aboard the train. When she had seated herself rather breathlessly in the coach just behind the one the boy had entered, she unfolded the bill.

"A hundred dollars!" she gasped. "Well, if this isn't a surprise. Where on earth—"

The train was moving now. Judy blew a kiss to her brother, who was watching from the station platform. Then she waved the bill to show him she appreciated it.

"Where on earth does he think I'm going?" she started to ask herself when, quite suddenly, it dawned upon her that she didn't know, herself.

Judy continued to stare at the hundred-dollar bill as if she had never seen one before. She knew Horace certainly wasn't in the habit of carrying that much money around. Probably he had intended to deposit it in the bank when they passed through Farringdon. If so, she had kept him so busy that he had forgotten to stop.

Her thoughts were interrupted by the conductor who was saying, "Tickets, please!"

"I'm sorry," Judy apologized, "but I didn't have time to buy a ticket."

"What about a reservation?"

"Do I need one?" she asked in dismay.

"If I do," she thought, "then the egg boy will, too."

"You do unless you intend to ride in the coaches all night. How far are you going?"

"To Chicago."

Judy knew she couldn't go any farther than that on this train. Long before they reached Chicago she hoped to have found out how far the egg boy was going.

"Where's your baggage?"

"I—I'll pick it up in Chicago," she stammered.

"Somebody meeting you there, eh."

Obviously the conductor took her to be younger than she was. In the candy-striped blouse with her auburn hair all loose and wind-blown about her face, she must look like a schoolgirl.

"Are there any empty seats in the car ahead?" she inquired as she handed the conductor her fare.

The seat she had taken was a hard one that faced backwards and offered a good excuse for her to move.

"There will be when we reach the next station. Is this the smallest you've got?"

He was regarding the big bill with suspicion.

Judy fished in her purse and found that with all her change she had enough. She put the hundred-dollar bill carefully away. Somehow, it made her uncomfortable.

"Relax, Judy!" she told herself. "You're on the train. Your fare's paid as far as Chicago and you're on the trail of the missing Harold Wilcox."

But she did not follow her own advice very well. When the conductor next passed through the train, she jumped to hear him speak directly to her.

"Better take that white ticket with you if you change seats here," he advised. "It's your receipt for the cash fare you paid."

"Thanks," murmured Judy, hurrying into the next car with the ticket in her hand.

Several people were getting off. Pretending to be looking for a seat, Judy searched among the remaining passengers until she recognized the boy she meant to follow. He was reading a comic book and did not look up as she passed his seat. The place next to him was already occupied by an elderly woman with an outrageous hat perched on top of graying blonde hair drawn back into a large bun.

"She must be getting off soon," Judy thought hopefully. "Otherwise she'd remove that hat."

After walking the length of the car and back again, Judy finally found a place across the aisle two seats behind the boy. From where she was sitting she could see only the top of his head.

"I won't do anything to attract his attention for a little while," she resolved. "But how I do wish I could read his thoughts!"

The purpose of this trip, she reminded herself, was neither to place the blame for Cleo Potter's loss on this boy nor to clear Holly of suspicion. That she might not be able to do without finding and opening the forbidden chest. Right now, the main thing was to help Peter solve his angle of the case.

Judy's Plan

"But I doubt if I can make the boy return willingly," she sighed, shaking her head over this last problem. It wasn't going to be easy!

Presently a porter came though the car with magazines and candy bars. Judy bought two comic books, intending to offer them to the boy in order to win his friendship. He bought a candy bar.

Afterwards Judy wished she had bought something to eat instead of wasting her money on the comic books. How could she share them or even speak to the boy without making it too obvious? She wasn't really hungry, though, as she had lunched late and did not mind skipping a meal. She had a double seat to herself and before very long she found herself nodding.

She awoke with a start as the train jerked to a stop at the next station. More people were crowding in.

"There must be seats somewhere," she heard a child's voice saying. "Here, Mommie! I've found one."

The little girl, who looked about six, had found the seat next to Judy.

"You may sit beside her if you like," Judy told the child's mother. "I'll find another place."

The place she had in mind was the seat next to Harold Wilcox. But when she looked for the boy she had been keeping in sight for so long, she knew a moment of real panic.

There was no dark head in sight across the aisle two seats in front of her!

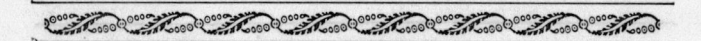

CHAPTER XIX

Destination Unknown

Judy's first impulse was to dash out at once in the hope of finding the boy, but this was impossible as the train had started again and was fast picking up speed.

As she made her way toward the seat she had been watching, she suddenly realized that it was still occupied. Soon she was laughing at her fears.

"What a scare I gave myself!" she thought. "And all for nothing."

The dark head was no longer in sight for the simple reason that it was now pillowed on the seat. The boy was sleeping soundly in a jackknife position, his feet on his suitcase. He had the double seat to himself, now,

Destination Unknown 147

but Judy decided not to disturb him. Instead, she took an unoccupied seat directly across the aisle from him.

"Now I can really keep him in sight," she told herself.

Adjusting her seat to a reclining position, she alternately dozed and watched the boy as the train sped on through the night.

In the morning Judy spent some time in the powder room making herself look as presentable as possible. The candy-striped blouse did not show wrinkles and her blue gabardine suit only needed brushing. Luckily, she had a pocket comb and makeup in her purse.

"You look all right," she finally told her reflection in the mirror. "Only you look—scared!"

Suddenly Judy realized that she not only looked, but actually was, a little scared. She had no idea what her destination might be or how many difficulties lay ahead of her. Suppose her plan didn't work and the boy refused to talk!

"He might be the silent type," she thought dubiously.

It proved to be the truth. He was still asleep when Judy returned to her seat, but awoke suddenly when the porter shouted through the car, "First call for breakfast!"

The boy sat up with a start, rubbed his eyes, and looked across at Judy.

"Did you have a good rest?" she inquired pleasantly.

At first he did not answer. But after a little he replied, "Fair," and picked up his comic book. If there was anything funny in it, his face did not show it. Soon he put it down in apparent distaste.

"Want to change?" Judy asked, offering him one of the comic books she had purchased.

"Sure, thanks!" He read a few pages and then said, "This is better than mine. You just got on, didn't you? I don't remember seeing you before."

That was all Judy wanted to know at the moment. Now it was safe to question him.

"People don't stay strangers very long on trains, or so I've heard," she began. "Are you traveling alone?"

That was a mistake. The boy was instantly on the defensive.

"Why not?" he asked. "I'm old enough."

She laughed.

"So am I."

"I'm glad there's someone young on the train," he volunteered. "My seatmate last night looked about eighty. She didn't smile, but if she had I'm sure it would have cracked her face."

"I was thinking the same of you until a minute ago," Judy admitted with a laugh. "Are you going into the dining car for breakfast?"

"I guess so. I'm starved!"

"So am I."

He didn't suggest that they go in together, but when

Judy arose to leave the car he followed her, holding open the doors for her in a manly way.

They ate in comparative silence. She had French toast, and he devoured a whole stack of pancakes. When the waiter put their checks on the table he paid them both.

"You shouldn't have done that," Judy protested.

"Why not?" he demanded. "I've got my own money and I guess I can spend it any way I want to."

"Thanks, anyway," Judy said. "It was a nice breakfast. I wonder if there'll be time for lunch in Chicago."

"Oh, lots," he replied. "That is, if you're taking the Overland. I am. It doesn't leave until eight o'clock. We have all afternoon."

"So he's taking the Overland," thought Judy. "That means I am, too."

"Are you going all the way across the country by coach?" she inquired.

"Sure," he replied. "Who wants to be bothered with a Pullman? I can sleep anywhere."

Judy smiled, but she didn't add, "Even in a cave, if necessary." Nor did she mention the mansion overlooking the blue Susquehanna. Didn't this boy yearn, just a little bit, for the comforts of his luxurious home?

"I'm going by coach, too," she said. "It's cheaper."

This was perfectly true. She was glad she would have so much time in Chicago. She'd spend it making telephone calls and assembling the necessary luggage for a cross-country trip. But would she have enough left for a ticket? And where was she going? It seemed so strange not to know.

"Say, what shall I call you?" her companion suddenly asked as they left the dining room together.

"Just Judy," she replied, still busy with her thoughts.

"You can call me Hal."

She started to ask if it was short for Harold, but stopped herself in time.

"I'll look for you on the Overland, Hal," she said a few hours later when the train pulled into Chicago.

"Okay, Judy. Be seeing you."

And he disappeared into the crowd that was milling about, for here in Chicago everybody had to change trains and, more often than not, be transported from one station to another by taxicab.

Judy had to stand a minute and catch her breath before she decided on her next move.

"It worked!" she told herself triumphantly. "The Wilcox boy and I are friends!"

Then she raced for a telephone and called Peter long distance to tell him the good news.

"It's really true," she informed him. "I'm on the trail of Harold Wilcox and what's more important, he likes me. He's taking the Overland and so am I. But so far I haven't been able to discover where he's going.

Peter, if he asks, I have to have a destination. What would you suggest?"

"I'll find one for you and send you a wire," he promised.

"On the train?"

"Of course. Where else? You're a wonder to do this for me, Angel," he added. "It took courage to board that train without having the least idea where you were going. Shall I tell the Wilcoxes their boy is safe?"

"Not yet," Judy advised. "They might mess things up if they knew. I guess Horace gave you all the details of our underground adventure. He loaned me a hundred dollars, Peter. It looked big until now. But if it has to pay my way clear across the country there won't be enough left to furnish myself with a traveling bag and a change of clothes."

"I'll wire the Chicago office and see that you have enough. Stop in and identify yourself and they'll hand it right over to you. Angel, I can't tell you how much I appreciate what you're doing—"

"Oh, Peter!" cried Judy, suddenly close to tears. "You—you're wonderful! Here I was all worried for fear it was the wrong thing, and now you make it all seem right. I do wish, though, that we could have been together on this trip. It's all so exciting and new, and I've always wanted to take a trip across the country with you."

"I'll fly out to meet you," Peter promised. "Will that do? Don't let that boy get away from you, though. We have to bring him home."

"What about his part in the robbery?"

"That still puzzles me," Peter admitted. "He seems to have played a part, to be sure. But there must be others involved. Organized gangsters who must have given him instructions. Find out about them, if you can. Win his confidence and get him to talk."

"I'll try, Peter." Judy hesitated. Then she said, "I have all afternoon in Chicago. Do you think there'll be time for me to visit Roberta after I go to the FBI office? I promised her that I would."

Peter thought it was a splendid idea and so it proved. The little girl who had boarded with Judy, before she followed the "Clue of the Stone Lantern" and discovered Roberta's real home, was delighted to see her. The child's mother solved the problem of Judy's luggage by offering to lend her two matching brown suitcases.

Judy liked brown. It made her hair seem less red. With what her hostess loaned her and the few extra purchases she made in Chicago, she had enough to fill the suitcases. Shopping for her strange trip, with the little girl she loved so dearly, turned out to be such fun that Judy nearly missed the Overland.

"That would have been a real calamity," she told herself when she was safely aboard the train.

She had to walk through several cars before she located her friend, Harold Wilcox. She really did have a friendly feeling for the boy now, and greeted him warmly.

"The rest of this trip is going to be a real adventure for me," she declared. "I have friends in Chicago, but I've never been any farther west."

"Neither have I. Will we go through cowboy country, do you think?"

"Your guess is as good as mine," she replied. "I'll be seeing everything for the first time. How far are you going?"

He evaded her question with another.

"How far are you?"

She laughed.

"You'll think this is funny, but I'm not sure of my destination until I receive a wire. It will be delivered to me on the train. My ticket takes me all the way through to San Francisco, but I'll probably stop off for a visit on the way. I'm returning by plane."

"You are?"

"Yes, how are you going back?"

"I'm not!"

His reply was so short that Judy asked no more questions until the following morning.

"Win his confidence," Peter had said.

But how was Judy going to do it?

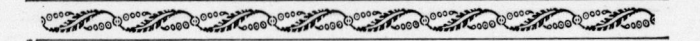

CHAPTER XX

The Prison Car

"What's happening?"

The question was directed to Judy. The boy who called himself Hal, and all the other passengers on the Overland were suddenly awake. They had arrived in Omaha, where there was so much switching and bumping that no one could possibly sleep.

Up to this point Judy had slept fairly well in her reclining seat with her head on a pillow she had rented for a quarter a night. Now she looked around in surprise to find the car nearly empty.

"I don't know what's happening," she replied. "I hope they aren't taking this car off the train. It certainly looks like it. Let's find out."

The Prison Car 155

Just then the conductor shouted, "All passengers please change to the car ahead."

Apparently this order had been given once before.

"It's crowded in there," one of the passengers came back from the car ahead to announce. "Isn't this car going through?"

"We're clearing it for prisoners," was the surprising reply.

"Prisoners!" exclaimed Hal, a look of fear crossing his face.

Another man, apparently a guard, came through.

"These seats have to be clear. We're bringing the men in now," he announced.

The seats he indicated were the four in the rear.

"I don't see why we can't stay where we are. He doesn't need the whole car for his prisoners, just the four rear seats," Judy whispered to the boy.

"But I don't want to ride in the same car with the cops," he protested.

Judy laughed.

"I think most of the passengers feel the other way about it. They don't want to ride in the same car with the prisoners. So it's the cops and not the prisoners that bother you?"

"Sure," he replied as the four men shuffled in. "I feel sorry for those guys. Probably they were framed."

"All passengers change to the car ahead—please!" the conductor shouted for the third time.

Judy noticed that everyone else had moved.

"We'd better do what he says," Hal insisted, picking up one of Judy's bags.

She picked up the remaining bag and tucked her pillow under her arm.

"Better take yours, too," she advised as they walked through to the next car. "We may still be able to get some sleep."

"Not me," he said. "I wish now I'd got off at Omaha, but the train's moving and it's too late."

"It certainly is," agreed Judy. "Anyway, what would you do in Omaha?"

"Get a job," he replied shortly. "I can work."

"I don't doubt that. You look like a good worker. Oh dear!" sighed Judy. "These seats are all taken. We'll have to try the next car."

But they had waited too long. There was not a seat to be found in the next car or the next one. After walking through four cars, they came at last to the diner and knew they could go no farther without disturbing the passengers in the Pullmans.

"Let's eat," the boy suggested. "Maybe someone will leave the train at the next station."

Judy agreed, but that didn't work either. They found the dining car deserted. It was still too early for breakfast. The sun was just rising over the flat prairie.

"Look!" Judy exclaimed as they stopped beside a

window. "Did you ever see the sky so beautiful before?"

The colors were almost too brilliant. At home the sky had never looked like this.

"It is pretty," Hall agreed. "It's prettier than the sunset. I don't usually get up this early, but I might as well get used to it. Cowboys have to get up early, don't they?"

"I suppose they do. Are you thinking of being a cowboy?" Judy asked.

"Why not?" Again he seemed to resent her question. "Do you think I couldn't ride?"

"Could you?" she asked.

"I could learn. I learn easily. I don't see any cowboys, though."

"Did you expect to see them galloping over the sagebrush the way they do on the screen?"

"And shooting," he added. "Did you?"

"Maybe," Judy laughed. "I did see a stock pen a short distance back—"

"Then this is cattle country! Maybe I'd better get off at the next station."

"What are you going to say when you're asked how much experience you've had?" asked Judy.

"Heck!" he exclaimed. "Everybody can't start with experience."

"I know. That does make it hard," Judy said with

real sympathy. "Come on. let's go back and try for seats again. We can't stand here gazing out the window all the way to California if that's where we're going. I noticed your ticket was to San Francisco, too."

"I couldn't go any farther. There's an ocean in the way."

And Hal laughed. The joke was one they could both appreciate. Judy wished she didn't like the boy so much. She would never forgive herself if she made life any harder for him than it was already.

"But life has been hard for Holly, too," she thought. "I don't believe either one of them is guilty!"

Saying this to herself, even though she had no facts on which to base her sudden conviction, made Judy feel better. Together she and Hal searched for seats with no more success than they had experienced before. Finally they found themselves back to the prison car. Judy pushed open the door.

"You can't come in here." A guard stopped her. "This is the prison car."

"I know," Judy said. "I spent the night here. We've looked all through the other cars and there aren't any seats. This car is nearly empty. I don't see why you couldn't let a few passengers ride in it. The prisoners don't need the whole car, do they?"

"They're dangerous criminals, lady."

"I know," she said sweetly, "but they have good strong guards to keep them from making trouble."

That did it.

"We-ll, I'll speak to my partner and see what he thinks," the guard said, and returned to where the other man was keeping watch over the sullen prisoners. A low conversation followed. There was much head-shaking and finally a nod of agreement.

"You win," the first guard said, returning to report on the conversation. "Sure you won't be frightened?"

"Of course not," Judy replied.

"How about your brother?"

Hal started to say something, but Judy broke in.

"Don't worry about him. He won't be afraid, either. And thanks—a lot!"

"Golly!" the boy exclaimed as they took their original places. "He thinks I'm your brother."

"That's convenient," Judy said. "I do have a brother, but he's older than you are. His name is Horace."

"Horace? That's even worse than Harold."

"They're both good names," declared Judy. After a moment she added, "A name is what you make it," and then watched his face.

For some time he stared fixedly at the prisoners, who were obviously not enjoying the ride. He had to turn around in his seat to see them. One of the guards shook his head, and Hal quickly looked the other way.

When the train stopped again, three more passengers were admitted to the car. Their friendly chatter encouraged Harold to talk more freely himself.

"Golly! I'd hate to be in their shoes," he said, his mind still on the prisoners.

"What made you say they probably were framed?" asked Judy.

"That's the way it's done," he returned as if speaking from experience. "I'll bet most of those guys wanted to do something good in the first place. Maybe they got jobs they thought were on the level and then got mixed up in something crooked without knowing it. The cops always catch up with the little guys first. Then, first thing they know, they have a prison record, and after that maybe they figure that crime is the only way out."

"But it isn't a way out. It's a way in—into prison," Judy said.

"I know that. I'm just telling you the way they might have figured it. They say once you've got a record, everyone is against you. Maybe they are anyway," he finished. "Lots of guys never have a chance."

"You mean because nobody believes in them?"

"That's about it."

"Don't your folks believe in you, Hal?"

"Aw, they think I'm just a kid," he declared. "They think I'm no good for anything. I figure some day I'll show them."

"How?" asked Judy.

His face clouded.

"That's just it," he said. "I don't know how. I tried the only thing I'm real good at, but it didn't work."

"What was that?" Judy questioned again, pretending no more than a friendly interest.

"Appraiser," he said. "That's what I'd like to be."

It was dawning upon Judy what he meant, but she spoke as if she did not understand.

"Do you mean you would like to appraise cattle and horses at auction?"

"Golly!" he exclaimed. "Do you think I could?"

"Maybe."

Judy was busy thinking. Appraiser? So that was what he wanted to be! It wasn't cattle and horses he wanted to appraise, though. It was antiques!

Armed with this information, Judy went in to breakfast with the boy, but made a condition.

"This time I pay the check. You're my kid brother."

"Okay," he agreed, "if you want to make a game of it. I do have to watch my spending. I've got twenty dollars left, but it won't last forever. Maybe we can buy crackers or something like that for lunch. It costs a lot to eat on the train."

Judy was discovering this herself. The breakfast check she paid made her even more aware of it. All morning the train carried her across the prairie toward her unknown destination. The scenery through the window became more and more barren. Gray hills that looked like ash heaps loomed in the distance. The prisoners were being served lunch trays from the diner. Harold dozed, his head on the window sill.

At last the train crossed into the State of Wyoming. Judy could just see the stone monument marking the boundary. At the capital city there was a twenty-minute stop and passengers were allowed to leave the train.

Harold awoke when the train stopped.

"Here's a chance to buy some provisions," Judy told him. "See if you can find something for me, too." And she handed him a dollar.

Crackers, milk in paper containers, fruit and candy were on sale in the station. While Harold shopped for food, Judy found a desk where she could send a telegram, and wired Peter:

> PLAN WORKING. BOY ADMITS NAME
> HAROLD. AMBITION TO BECOME AP-
> PRAISER. WANTS WORK ON RANCH.
> STILL WAITING FOR DESTINATION.
> LOVE
> JUDY

She did not mention the prison car.

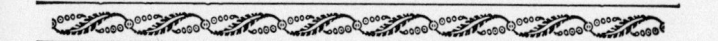

CHAPTER XXI

A Full Confession

"Where were you?" asked Harold as Judy joined him after a breathless dash for the train.

"I was nearly left behind," she panted.

"I'm glad you weren't. I mean what were you doing to keep you so long? I was afraid I'd have to eat all this food by myself."

"I was sending a telegram," she replied truthfully. "After all, I would like to know where I'm going."

He grinned in appreciation.

"We're both in the same boat, I guess. You aren't running away from home, are you?"

"Do I look like a runaway?" she asked, trying his tactics.

"Not exactly," he replied, "but you do look sort of bewildered."

"And no wonder!" she exclaimed. "I'm supposed to visit someone on my way to San Francisco, but I forgot to find out where to get off the train. They allow you a stop-over, you know. The ticket's good for a month."

"It is?"

"Yes, it's printed right here. See?"

She pointed out the fine print on the ticket she had purchased in Chicago, and he read it thoughtfully. As they lunched on the food he had bought, everything was so peaceful, they quite forgot the prisoners. Outside the scenery had changed again. The train had now ascended to the highest point on the route. From this altitude the mountain tops were so impressive that they looked almost unreal.

"They make you feel as if you're on another planet, don't they?" asked Judy.

Harold nodded.

"I like the scenery back home better. This is too bare. Most of the time there isn't a green thing in sight. It sure will look good to see shade trees and green lawns again."

"I thought you weren't going back."

"Oh, I will some time when I've made good. Maybe I'll call up from San Francisco. I could reverse the charges. Mom and Dad may be worried about me."

A Full Confession 165

"I would," Judy advised. "Tell me about your home, Hal. What's it like?"

He hesitated, then answered without looking at Judy.

"Like everyone else's, I guess. Living room, dining room, knickknacks around."

He was describing the homes on his egg route, not his own, Judy realized.

"My home is like that, too," Judy said, "only we have a big kitchen and no dining room. We eat by the front window where we can look out at the brook and the green trees. And in the corner is a beautiful old china closet filled with antiques my grandmother left me. I love antiques, don't you?"

"I used to, but now I hate them," he declared with sudden violence. "You ought to lock them up where they can't be stolen. I'll bet lots of the stuff you see in antique shows is spotted in homes like yours by some innocent guy who has no idea it's going to be taken. The thieves get away with it, too, because the little guy is there to get the blame. He's trapped and can't get out of it, even after he knows it's crooked. Like those poor guys in the back of this car. They probably got the blame while some big fellow sat back and collected the dough—or the antiques. It's all the same as far as I'm concerned, and I'm through with the lot of them!"

"Well!" Judy said in surprise when he had finished. "That was quite a speech. But how do you know it's true?"

"Of course it's true. Okay," he said recklessly, "you're a stranger. When this trip is over I'll probably never see you again, and I've got to talk to somebody. Judy, I wanted to be an appraiser, and I don't mean cattle. I wanted to find out the value of the treasures people keep in their homes. You know, sort of tell them what the things their grandparents left them are worth in money. I studied hard and learned how to do it, too. I thought I could make my father proud of me. You see, he—he values such things. I—I guess I wanted to impress him. But what happened?"

"What did?" asked Judy

"Nothing happened—to me," he replied abruptly. "I got out in time and I'm going to stay out. This is the last time I'll ever ride in a prison car—"

"But you're only a passenger," Judy protested.

He sighed.

"You'll never know how close I came to being back there with those fellows. If I hadn't happened to pick up the paper— But why am I telling you all this? You don't care. I'm just a boy you'll never see again, and—well, for all anybody cares about me, I might as well be dead."

"Hal, please!" begged Judy. "Don't say such things. To hear you talk, anybody might think you'd been in serious trouble."

"I was," he replied. "That's what I've been telling you. The man who got me into it is a friend of my father's and an appraiser himself. He's known all over the country, and if I told people he was nothing but a crook, do you think they'd believe me? He said he was interested in my ambitions. He listened to everything I told him. He promised he was going to help me. 'Keep your eyes open and tell me what you see,' he said, and so I kept my eyes open and told him. And what do you think he did? Last Wednesday he gave me a lift outside of school to a house where I was delivering something. I saw some nice stuff in there and I told him so when I found he'd been waiting for me in his car around the corner. He made me get in and go with him to pick up another man. Then we went back to this house, and he told me to sit in the car with him and watch to see if the people who lived there were coming home. And the other man went in and took all the antiques I'd told about!"

Judy gasped. Harold looked at her without expression and then went on: "When he came out, I asked them what was the idea, and they told me to keep my mouth shut or they'd see that I was blamed for the robbery.

"I was in so deep, I was scared to go home that night," Harold continued. "So I went to a—to a secret place I know. But when I saw in the paper that the cops were looking for me, I knew I had to get right out of town. Judy," Harold finished vehemently, "I never stole a thing, but who'll ever believe me?"

"I will," said Judy. "If you say you never touched the antiques—"

"I touched them, of course. An appraiser has to. But I never took a thing."

Judy was convinced that the boy was telling the truth. But what about Holly? Holly, who had chided her for suspecting an innocent egg boy, little dreaming that she herself would be suspected. Or had she known it? Judy remembered her haste, the clanking sound like pieces of glassware rattling around in their hiding place. Had Holly told the truth about the forbidden chest? Certainly she had not told it with the sincerity and directness of this boy. Somehow, believing him made Judy doubt her friend all over again.

"It's made me feel better to tell you anyway, Judy," Harold was saying. "Golly, this country is big!" he added, gazing out the window. "It seems as if we'd been riding forever."

"It does, doesn't it? Look!" Judy exclaimed. "There's one of those flat-topped red rocks I've seen in pictures! And there's a real cave. Don't you just love caves?"

"I used to," he admitted, "but I wouldn't want to hide out in one all my life. Would you?"

"I wouldn't hide out," she replied. "I'd talk, just the way you've done. No matter what happens, if you speak right out and tell the truth, you're on the winning side."

A Full Confession

Harold just looked at her and then turned toward the window. The train was entering the red desert. Nobody spoke for a little while except to exclaim over the scenery. Rocks in all colors of the rainbow rose above the tracks. The fantastic buttes, as they were called by the other passengers, continued in view until it became too dark for them to be seen. After another meal in the dining car with her "brother," Judy rented a fresh pillow and slept for the third night on the train.

In the middle of the night she was awakened by a noise from the back of the car. If one of the prisoners had become violent, he was soon subdued. But now Judy could detect a strangeness in the air. The train was passing over the long causeway across Great Salt Lake. She peered through the window but could see so little of the lake that she resolved to take the trip again and cross it in the daytime.

More passengers had been admitted to the prison car until now it was nearly as full as the others. Harold awoke, called out something about a hideout, and promptly went to sleep again. But Judy stayed awake until nearly morning.

"Where is the telegram Peter promised me?" she kept wondering.

Surely he had received her own telegram by now. It practically demanded a reply. What could have happened?

"I'll telephone home from San Francisco and try and

persuade Harold to do likewise," she decided and finally fell asleep again.

It was broad daylight when she awoke.

"Hi, Sis!" Harold called across to her. He had been talking with the other passengers while waiting for her to accompany him into the dining car. He seemed to enjoy the pretend game of being her brother.

"I figure that if we eat breakfast late we can skip lunch again. What do you think?" he asked.

Judy laughed. "It's okay with me. You're always figuring something, aren't you? Just in case we get hungry I'll pop the extra breakfast rolls they're sure to give us into my bag. Have you any idea what state we're in?"

"Nevada," he said.

Judy frowned. She was thinking of Peter and the telegram. Why didn't he send it? How was she going to bring Harold home if he didn't? What was she going to do?

"You look worried," Harold remarked over the breakfast table.

"I am," declared Judy. "I never got that telegram. I'll have to telephone home from San Francisco and find out where to go."

The boy shook his head.

"I wish I could solve all my problems with a telephone call. Maybe I should have done what you said,

A Full Confession

told the truth in the first place, instead of running away."

"You can always go back, can't you?"

"On twenty dollars?" he asked. "No, I have to find a job and prove to my folks that I'm good for something. If you hear of one, let me know."

"I sure will," agreed Judy, "and if you run across a telegram—"

Just then the waiter came to their table with the check.

"People do receive telegrams on trains, don't they?" Judy asked him.

"Sure thing," he replied. "The conductor was calling one through the dining car yesterday. You'll get it all right if anyone sends you a telegram on this train."

"Thank you," said Judy, leaving him a tip and accepting the fresh napkin he gave her. He had noticed that she was helping herself to the extra rolls, but merely grinned to say he understood.

"You know there's one thing you get on trains," Harold confided as they walked back through the cars to their own seat. "It's a good feeling, as if the whole of this big country is full of friends. It's fun making the other passengers think we're brother and sister, isn't it? I wish—"

"What do you wish?" asked Judy when he hesitated.

"I wish we were."

Judy felt sudden tears in her eyes. It was impossible not to think of the end of the trip when Harold must surely learn the truth. Would he hate her for following him and pretending?

"Judy, you're crying!" he suddenly observed.

"I didn't mean to," she apologized. "It's just because the trip is almost over and—"

"You didn't get that telegram," he finished. "But it doesn't matter. You can telephone home. I'll wait until you're sure everything's all right."

"What about you?" asked Judy. "Are you going to telephone?"

"Maybe. Let's look at the scenery. See that river way down there in the gorge below the tracks? It's like a silver thread."

"You should see it in the spring when the snow on these mountains is melting. It's a raging torrent then," one of the passengers sitting near them volunteered. "Keep watch on your side of the train. Pretty soon we'll come to Donner Lake. If you ever think you have troubles—"

And the passenger, a stout middle-aged woman who looked as if she had never known the pangs of hunger, went on to relate the story of the emigrant band who had been left snowbound and starving by the lake. It was a tragic tale and left Judy feeling worse, if anything, than she had felt before.

All afternoon the mountain scenery was too impres-

A Full Confession

sive to miss. Judy didn't move from her seat. From the ridge above the deepest canyon, she could look across a hundred miles of mountains. Then gradually the train descended from the heights into a broad valley where the fields were golden in the sunshine and orchards were heavy with fruit. Harold was inspired by the sight.

"I could get a job picking fruit," he said.

But Judy begged him to stay on the train with her a little longer. She was feeling panicky now. Where would she go? What would she do when the trip was ended?

"I've been expecting a telegram," she told the conductor the next time he entered the car.

"A telegram!" he exclaimed. "Your name isn't Judy—?"

"It is!" she cried. "Did the telegram come?"

"It came yesterday," he replied, fishing in his pocket for it. "I called it through every car . . ."

"Except this one," thought Judy. She was sure he had not called the telegram through the prison car.

Unfolding the yellow slip of paper, she read with increasing amazement:

> UNCLE JOHN EXPECTS YOU BOTH. IF YOU MISS
> HIM TAKE TAXI TO WILD HORSE RANCH. GET OFF
> AT CROCKETT. PD

CHAPTER XXII

At Wild Horse Ranch

"THIS is the strangest telegram I ever received. Where's Crockett?" asked Judy as the conductor started to leave the car. "I'm supposed to get off there."

"You're too late," he replied. "We passed through there half an hour ago, but you can get off at Berkeley and take the next train back. It's due in twenty minutes."

"Thank you," said Judy, still looking bewildered.

"What's wrong?" asked Harold.

"Everything," Judy declared, showing him the telegram. "I was supposed to get off this train half an hour ago."

"Who's PD?" he asked curiously.

At Wild Horse Ranch 175

Judy knew Peter had signed only his initials, according to a secret agreement they had once made, to indicate a double meaning to his message.

"Don't worry," she replied. "It's not 'Police Department.' It's just a relative. I've never met Uncle John. I hope he knows me—if he's still there."

"It says he expects you both," Harold observed. "What does that mean?"

Judy sighed.

"The telegram isn't very clear, is it? I guess he thought my brother was with me."

"Could I—" Harold began nervously, and then broke off. "No, I guess I couldn't. He'd know I wasn't your brother."

"I don't see how," Judy replied. "He's never seen Horace either. It's a long way across the country, as we've just discovered. Neither of us has ever visited him."

"Do you mean—Judy, you can't mean it's all right if I go to the ranch with you!"

"Of course it's all right. Please do," she begged. "I'm scared to death. I may have missed Uncle John, and I wouldn't know him from Adam, anyway, and if he's looking for two of us he may not know me either, Oh! Here we are at Berkeley!"

Harold had to come to a decision quickly.

"Okay," he said, "I'm with you."

They assembled their baggage near the door as it

was opened. One of the prisoners smiled and Judy smiled back, and included all the friends they had made in the good wishes she called as they left the car.

After they had crossed the tracks to wait for the train that would take them back to Crockett, Harold admitted that it would have looked queer if he had remained aboard the train when the other passengers as well as the conductor believed he was Judy's brother.

"I hope it will be just as easy to fool Uncle John, whoever he is," he finished.

"All I hope is that he's there," declared Judy.

She did not need to pretend bewilderment. No doubt Peter knew what he was doing when he sent such a strange telegram, but she certainly didn't. Uncle John, in all probability, was another FBI agent like Peter himself. Maybe Peter had arranged everything so they would have a place to meet and talk things over with Harold before returning him to his own people. But Wild Horse Ranch! It sounded like pioneer days rather than present-day California.

Soon the train came clanging in and, in a very short time, it had brought them back to Crockett. The town was practically in a nest formed by the surrounding hills.

"They're not like the hills at home," Harold observed. "Everything is brown."

"Oh dear!" Judy exclaimed as they entered the station. "There isn't anyone here to meet us."

"There was a man here with four little kids not more than ten minutes ago," the station agent informed her. "He was looking for someone by the name of Judy—"

"I'm Judy! When will he be back?"

"He didn't say. Maybe he figured you didn't come."

"Then where can I find a taxi that will take us to Wild Horse Ranch?"

"Let me see now." The man behind the window pondered her question. "Maybe you'd better take a bus to Napa and get your taxi there. I don't know exactly where the ranch is, but it must be somewhere in Wild Horse Valley. Named for pioneer times when cowboys used to capture wild horses there. I reckon they're all tame now."

"Not too tame, I hope. It would be fun to capture a wild one," Harold said unexpectedly.

"Well, you may have the chance. The boys were saying something about a colt that needed training. But you can ask them about it yourself. Here they come back again!"

A tall, blue-eyed, angular man wearing blue jeans and a wide-brimmed hat opened the station door at that very moment. With him were four children, two little towheaded girls and two boys who looked about ten and twelve.

"Well, here you are!" he exclaimed before Judy could recover from her surprise. "I'm your uncle John and these are your cousins Larry, Michael, Susie, and

Tina. She's so tiny that we shortened Kristina's name. Come and shake hands with your cousins, children. This is Judy and her brother Horace—"

"He doesn't like the name Horace," Judy explained quickly. "We call him Hal."

"Well, why not, if that's the way he wants it," boomed this amazing new uncle. "Come on, the car's waiting. It's a lucky thing we came back here. I thought we'd missed you."

"We went past our station," Judy explained, wondering all the time how long this play-acting could be kept up. Surely these wide-eyed children knew Judy and the boy who was pretending to be her brother weren't their real cousins!

"How did that happen?"

Harold explained about the prison car and the telegram that almost hadn't been delivered.

"I guess those guys were on their way to the Rock," he finished. "They looked awful glum."

"And why not? Prison's no picnic. I'm surprised that you were allowed to ride in the same car with them."

Uncle John's voice was more serious now.

"He *is* an FBI man," thought Judy, but the elaborate pretense continued to amaze her.

The ride to Wild Horse Ranch was a pleasant change from the train. They crossed a long bridge over the bay area of Crockett and were soon driving up into the

At Wild Horse Ranch   179

brown hills. This was the dry season, Uncle John explained.

"You should see these hills in the spring when they're dotted with wild flowers and everything is green."

"It must be a beautiful sight," agreed Judy. "The orchards must be pretty, too. This is fruit-raising country, isn't it?"

"Yes, but we raise cattle, too. The boys won prizes for their steers last year. They're real cowboys, not the rootin' tootin' kind you see on the screen. You ride, of course."

This was not a question. It was a statement which neither Judy nor Harold felt called upon to answer. Whatever else Uncle John was or was not, he must certainly be the father of these four children. He seemed so proud of them.

It was growing dark by the time they came to a huge sign posted on a live oak tree:

WILD HORSE RANCH

Here a narrow road turned off the main highway. Trees heavy with prunes grew on one side. On the other was what the boys called irrigated pasture. Two horses were grazing there. The boys wanted to show them off and rode ahead of the car the rest of the way to the house.

Beyond the house, which was low and flat, Judy could just see the barn with its white trim and the white fence posts. Or was that a fence post? Suddenly it whinnied.

"Is that a *horse?*" asked Judy.

It had sounded more like the wailing of a banshee.

"It's a colt," Susie spoke up. "Drive on up to the barn and let them see it, Daddy."

Judy took one look at the colt and shuddered. She had never seen anything like it.

"What is it," she asked, "an albino?"

"Almost. It will be Susie's when the boys get it trained," Uncle John explained. "She's named it Baby Blue Eyes."

The creature actually did have eyes that were a clear light blue. Otherwise it was all white with a pinkish tint about its nose and what Tina called "a mad look" in its face.

"Watch out! It may bite you," Uncle John cautioned when Harold tried to pet it.

"I'll ride that colt tomorrow," he told Judy grandly, as they walked back toward the house.

"I wouldn't try it if I were you," she protested. "I rode a colt once just to show off and it nearly threw me in the path of a speeding train. The colt's name was Ginger. He's still a spirited horse and I still ride him occasionally. My brother does, too. I hope—"

Here Judy's voice was drowned out in a clamor from the house.

At Wild Horse Ranch

"Our cousins are here! Is supper ready, Mom?" the children were calling.

A pleasant-faced woman in a large apron bustled out on the porch and greeted Judy and Harold with a hearty "Well, so my sister's children have come to visit their aunt Helen at last. I'm delighted to meet you."

"I'm glad to know you, too, Aunt—Helen."

Judy knew, of course, that her mother had no sister. She hoped to find out who these people really were before they carried things too far. It was going to be quite a trick for her to remember so many new names.

"I'm flabbergasted," she confessed later to Harold. "I never knew I had all these relatives."

"What about me? They're taking me right in as if I belonged here. That was a swell meal they dished out, wasn't it? Judy, I don't know how I can ever thank you—"

"Thank me for what?" thought Judy. "For leading you into a trap? Can't you see that we're all pretending?"

Aloud she said, "Don't try," and hurried away to be shown to her room by "Aunt" Helen.

"No questions tonight, dear," she was told before she'd even had a chance to ask any. That meant, of course, that there would be no answers, either. Still bewildered and more than a little apprehensive, Judy finally fell asleep to be awakened at the crack of dawn with excited squeals.

"We're going to the auction!"

The auction wasn't until afternoon but, somehow, it took all morning to get ready for it.

"Hal wants to be an appraiser," Judy confided to the oldest boy. "What kind of an auction is it?"

She had hoped it would be an auction of antiques. But Larry answered, "They auction off livestock. Hal will sure have to learn a lot. I can't understand that lingo myself."

At the auction Judy learned what he meant. Everybody sat around the corral where the cattle and horses were brought in. As each one was offered for sale, the appraiser called out in a voice that only the cattle men understood. Signs passed between them, a raised finger, the nod of a head, and the bidding was over.

"You'll never get it," Harold was informed by the two boys. "Dad's going to buy some calves to raise. Watch him! He's bidding now."

Their father jerked his head slightly as a pair of spotted calves were offered for sale.

"They're ours," Larry announced, understanding the gesture that interrupted the steady drone of the auctioneer.

"We'll have to auction off the colt, Dad says, if we can't break him ourselves," Michael spoke up. "He's been a lot of trouble. We have to shut him in the barn

At Wild Horse Ranch

whenever we ride the horses, to keep him from jumping the fence and running after his mother. Once, when Larry was riding her past the barn, Baby Blue Eyes jumped right through the window. The glass cut him so badly we had to have the vet to fix him up. He's still got the scars, so he won't be worth much."

"I'll break him for you," Hal offered.

The boys took him at his word. They had no sooner arrived home with the calves than the colt was brought out into the pasture. Judy did not realize what was happening until she heard excited yells.

"Jump him when he's not looking!" the boys were shouting.

It came back to Judy in a flash that Harold had said on the train that he did not know how to ride. He must be stopped! But she was too late. Before she could reach the spot the children had chosen for their rodeo, as they called it, Hal was already mounted and they were perched on the top rail of the pasture fence, cheering him on.

"Grab him by the neck, Hal! Don't let him throw you!" Larry and Michael were shouting as the colt tried to shake the determined boy off his back.

Baby Blue Eyes rolled his pale eyes with their weird fringe of white lashes, and snorted warningly. Then he bucked. Harold's grip on the animal's neck tightened. He was riding bareback, as the colt had never worn a saddle.

"He's showing him who's boss all right," the boys called out to Judy, who was running toward them. "Hold on for dear life, Hal! That's the way to ride him!"

All four children were cheering. But their cheers turned to shrieks as the colt reared on his hind legs and then came down with such force that Harold shot over his head like a bullet and landed in the grass almost at Judy's feet.

Judy acted quickly. She was not quick enough to save Harold from a hard fall, but she was in time to throw herself at the enraged colt who might have trampled him in another moment. Surprised by this onslaught from a different quarter, Baby Blue Eyes meekly backed away.

Meantime the children, sobered by the accident, had climbed down from the fence and were now gazing at Harold with mixed awe and admiration.

The boy had not moved. Judy bent over him fearfully.

"Harold!" she called, in her anxiety forgetting that he was supposed to be Horace.

The children came closer to peer at him.

"Is the game over?" asked Tina.

"All over, I'm afraid," sighed Judy. "Run to the house and get your mother and father. Ask them to call a doctor. This boy is badly hurt!"

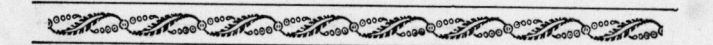

CHAPTER XXIII

Questions and Answers

"Is he—"

"He is going to be all right," the doctor assured the anxious group waiting as he came out of the room where the boy had been carried after the accident.

Peter was among them. He had simply come to the door and knocked as if he were a neighbor dropping in, instead of an FBI agent who had flown clear across the country to take home a boy who reportedly had been kidnaped. He had arrived just ahead of the doctor, and Judy had rushed into his arms and sobbed out all her fears against his coat.

His arm was still around her as they anxiously awaited the doctor's verdict.

"Are there any—bones broken?" Judy inquired.

"No, but his arm is badly bruised. He will have to keep it in a sling for a few days. He was pretty well shaken up generally. I wouldn't recommend any more riding," the doctor finished.

"He was good, though," Larry declared, "plenty good. Don't you kind of wish he was our real cousin, Mike?"

"I sure do," the younger boy replied.

"He broke the colt like he said he would. Now Baby Blue Eyes is mine," announced Susie.

"Don't—" The voice came from the boy in the bedroom. Harold had been listening. "Tell her not to ride him until he's really trained," he called. "That colt isn't—safe!"

"I know. Oh, Hal, I'm so sorry!" cried Judy, hurrying in to him. "I should have stopped you, but you were so brave—"

"I was a fool to try it," he declared, gazing ruefully at his bandages. "And I was a fool to be taken in by your trick. Even these kids knew it was a trick. You trailed me here! You were the redheaded girl in that car that banged into the man who drove me to Binghamton. I saw you when you ducked out of sight. It's just come back to me."

Judy's reply was a surprised gasp. She had dreaded the moment when he would find her out, and now it had come. Then she remembered that Peter had come, too, and that made it easier.

Questions and Answers 187

"I've been figuring it all out just now, lying here," Harold continued bitterly. "All this cousin business was nothing but a trap! I suppose I ought to thank you for stopping the colt, but I'd be better off if you'd let it kill me. You know," he finished weakly, "I—I can't sit up."

"Don't try," begged Judy. "You're badly bruised. Where do you hurt?"

"All over," he said. "Mostly inside. Maybe it's just the bruises. I don't know. The doctor says I'll feel better tomorrow, but I'm not ever going to feel better about the trick you played on me. You never meant what you said on the train—about telling the truth—"

"But I did mean it," protested Judy. "Harold, you've figured things all wrong. Sometimes a person has to use strategy to get at the truth, but you can still have faith in it. You'll be glad you told me—"

"Like I'm glad I fell off the colt?" he interrupted sarcastically. "I'll be tickled pink when it all comes out in the papers that Harold Wilcox is the 'mystery boy' the police were looking for. That'll fix me good with my folks, won't it? They'll be ashamed to own me—"

"Nonsense!" Judy stopped him. "They'll be proud."

"Of what? That I'm a thief?"

"But you're not," she reminded him. "You told me yourself that you were innocently involved. They're going to be proud of what you've learned, of your interest in your father's hobby, of your determination to make something of yourself, of your independence, of your courage, of—of everything! Besides, your name won't be in the paper unless you want it there. Peter, come here!" Judy called to him. "I want you to meet Harold Wilcox. Peter Dobbs is with the FBI, Harold, and he wants to thank you for your cooperation. You're helping solve at least two mysteries."

"I am?"

"Yes, you really are. One is the mystery of the stolen antiques, and the other is your own disappearance. Your parents thought you had been kidnaped, and asked Peter to find you."

"But you know him," the boy charged. "You were glad to see him. I heard you when he came in."

"Why shouldn't I be glad to see him?" asked Judy. "He's the 'PD' who signed that telegram I showed you on the train. I told you he was a relative, but I didn't mention that he is my husband."

"Your husband! Jeepers, are you married? I thought you were still in high school."

"She was, not so long ago," Peter declared. "It's true, Harold. Your parents asked me to find you. At first they wouldn't believe you had run away. They thought they'd given you everything and made you perfectly happy. They were sure you'd been kidnaped until I pointed out a few things that might not have been so perfect from your point of view. Things will be different from now on, you may be sure. They don't blame you for running away, Harold. They blame themselves."

"But jeepers, it wasn't their fault."

"They think it was. And they are going to be proud of you. You're going to help us find the real robbers and locate the antiques Holly was accused of stealing—"

"Who's Holly?" asked Harold, beginning to show an interest in Peter's proposal.

"She's a friend of Judy's. A very mysterious friend, I might add."

Questioned about her, Judy told Harold how he had interrupted the reading of Holly's story when he knocked at the door, and how it had seemed particularly strange because of her uncanny ability to look into the past.

"She's about your age," Judy informed him. "In fact, a little younger. She won't be sixteen until Christmas. You'd like her, Harold. She's interested in antiques, too. This story she's writing is about a glass blower's daughter. But Holly's cousin accused her of stealing her glassware."

"The poor kid!" Harold sympathized. "I know just how she feels."

"An antique brass chest that she refuses to open made things look bad for her," Judy continued. "She calls it the forbidden chest. You may have seen it."

Harold started up eagerly, then sank back wincing. "Sure, I know the chest you mean," he said. "While I was waiting for the girl to find out—say, was that Holly?" he asked curiously.

Judy nodded.

"Didn't she *ever* open the chest?" he asked wonderingly.

"No, she says her mother forbade it. She died when Holly was quite young, and as this was her last command Holly has never disobeyed it. The temptation would be too much for me," Judy admitted. "I'm full of curiosity, especially since the chest disappeared—"

"Was it stolen?" asked Harold.

"We're afraid so. We don't know what else could have happened to it. Perhaps you can help us get it back."

"I'll sure try," Harold promised. "Maybe I was wrong about you at that, Judy. I'm beginning to get your idea. But how do these make-believe cousins fit, and who are they anyway?"

"I've been wondering that myself," Judy confessed. "Is 'Uncle John' another FBI man, Peter?"

"No, he's just been cooperating with the FBI, like Harold here. You were cooperating, Harold, when you told Judy the truth. I'd promised your folks to bring you home, but it was rather important to find out why you'd left before I did so," Peter explained. "I know now, and so will they when they hear your story."

"Will they believe it? Mr. King was their friend—"

"*Was* is right," Peter said. "He won't be, much

Questions and Answers

longer. By the way, your father has an invitation for you. It's to the Collector's Club dinner. When I told him you wanted to be an appraiser, the men decided to make the next meeting Father and Son night. I promised him you'd be there."

"Will I!" exclaimed Harold, forgetting that he couldn't sit up. "Couldn't we fly home?"

The plane trip had to wait only long enough for the worst of Harold's bruises to heal. A week later, after bidding good-bye to their make-believe relatives at Wild Horse Ranch, he and Judy and Peter were off for Oakland. Their plane left from there, flying straight across the country to New York.

"We never got to San Francisco," Judy sighed as they climbed aboard the luxurious silver plane. "But this will be quite a change from the prison car."

"The prison car?" questioned Peter.

Judy giggled.

"Didn't we tell you? Harold and I rode in the car with four men on their way to prison. They looked so dejected that I guess they scared him into telling me—"

"I could imagine myself in their shoes," the boy admitted. "I thought the little guys were the ones who always got caught. It never entered my head that I might help trap the real criminal."

"And clear Holly of suspicion," Judy added happily.

CHAPTER XXIV

When the Chest Was Opened

AFTER a fast trip which Harold declared he would never forget, the plane circled at last over the runway at La Guardia Field in New York. As it settled gently to earth, two men wheeled a portable stairway to the cabin door and the passengers began to descend.

"Judy! Peter!" a familiar voice hailed them.

And there was Holly, of all people, with a whole group of their friends from Farringdon and Roulsville!

"Lois drove me here. We're all going to the antique show," she announced. "Wouldn't it be fun if we could spot some of the stolen antiques?"

"That's what Harold was saying. I want you to meet—"

When the Chest Was Opened 193

But, as Judy turned to introduce him, the boy darted through the crowd. He had seen his mother and father!

"Harold, my boy!" Judy heard Mr. Wilcox exclaim, his voice husky.

Tears were streaming down the face of the boy's mother as he clasped her in his arms and reassured her that he was home to stay.

Judy watched them, smiling. Then she turned back to her friends.

"If I'd known we were going to the antique show," she said, "I might have brought my strawberry plate along to be appraised."

"I wish you had!" exclaimed Peter's sister Honey, who was there with Horace and Donald Carter, another reporter from the *Farringdon Daily Herald*.

"I do, too," Lois chimed in. "The appraiser is the celebrated Mr. Stanislaus R. King!"

"We have a little surprise for him," Peter announced grimly. "Whether or not we find any stolen antiques at the show, I'm going to ask Harold to make a formal identification of him. And then I have a few questions I'm going to ask Mr. King to answer in Harold Wilcox's presence."

"May we listen?" the two reporters asked in the same breath.

Peter's questions were brief and to the point. To make sure he got the right answers, two New York detectives accompanied him. They soon hustled the appraiser out of the antique show in a less dignified manner than he had entered. After that, Judy and her friends turned their attention to the matter of locating the stolen antiques. The few they found were being exhibited by dealers who believed they had come by them honestly.

"There's the angel clock!" Judy pointed out excitedly as they walked past an especially attractive exhibit.

With them was Harold Wilcox, who had joined in the search and identified a number of stolen articles that were being exhibited by Brandt's Antique Department, of Farringdon. They had purchased them, the exhibitor reported, from a wholesale antique dealer by the name of Jack Hauser.

"No wonder he and Mr. King didn't want to be seen together," was Judy's comment.

The antique show was being held at Madison Square Garden, and occupied so much space that it took a lot of walking just to see everything. At first it was exciting, then tiring, and finally just discouraging.

"We'll never locate everything this way," declared Lois. "Let's leave it to Peter and the police, and start home. Harold left with his parents half an hour ago."

"I did hope we'd find the Millville Rose or some of the glassware Holly was accused of stealing," Judy said, and added to herself, "or the forbidden chest."

Where could it be, she wondered. What was in it, and why had it been forbidden in the first place?

When the Chest Was Opened 195

These three questions continued to perplex Judy, but it was not until a week later that she decided they simply had to be answered. The police had located the antiques stolen in all five robberies—with the exception of Cleo Potter's blue glass hen dish and the Millville Rose.

Now Judy was home again and things were beginning to fall back into their old routine. She was dishing out mash for the hens, a very ordinary task, when she recognized a car that had just turned down the North Hollow road as the one belonging to Fred Potter, Holly's cousin. His wife, Cleo, was beside him in the front seat.

"Here comes trouble," Judy whispered. "Good-bye, chick-a-biddies, I feel I'm needed elsewhere."

Leaving them to gorge themselves on the mash, she dashed along the short cut until she reached her neighbors' home. Blackberry, who had become a little jealous of the attentions the chickens were receiving, followed her.

Judy was just in time. As she approached the house, she could hear Cleo's rasping voice through the open door.

"This is your last chance to tell me the truth, Holly! I reported you once, and I'll report you again. I'll admit the clock and the other things were stolen by those two awful men, but the police have found no trace of the Millville Rose or my blue glass hen. Mrs. Ott got back all of her valuables—all of them! So did Mrs. Vaughn, and Mrs. Blessing, and I would have gotten back all mine too, if my own—"

She stopped as Judy appeared in the doorway.

"Yes, I'm here again, black cat and all," Judy said in answer to the suprised look Cleo Potter gave her. "So I traveled all the way across the country and still didn't clear Holly of suspicion! Well, I guess the only way to do it is to find the forbidden chest. And when we do, we're going to open it!"

"But Judy, it's disappeared—" Holly began.

"Look, Holly," Judy said, "you don't want to go through life being suspected of something you didn't do, do you? I think *you* made the chest disappear, yourself! And if you did, you can bring it back. You don't need to open it. *I'll* open it. Then we'll soon prove to your cousin that her missing antiques aren't in it. How about it, Holly?"

"How—how did you know—" Holly stammered. Then she said, "I guess I should have known I couldn't fool anyone as clever as you are, Judy. At least, not for long. Did you know I hid it, all the time?"

"Not at first," Judy said. "But when I really began using my head, I knew it couldn't have been anyone else but you. Is there a secret door of some kind in your study?"

"No, only the bookshelves. They move—"

"They didn't budge for me," Judy protested.

When the Chest Was Opened

"It takes two to move them," Holly explained. "Someone has to unlatch them and push from behind the wall. Uncle David helped me hide the chest. He could see I didn't want to open it, and so he left the room and slipped quietly upstairs. He came down the ladder behind the wall and swung open the bookshelves. Then he lowered the chest into that tunnel he had dug. You know, the one you discovered before."

"The one Blackberry showed me? So the bookshelves open into it, too!"

"They're part of the wall where the ladder goes down from my uncle's room. But, Judy, Uncle David didn't make me open the chest. And I'm still afraid of what may be in it. How do I know something won't happen to *you* if you open it?"

"To me?" Judy asked in surprise.

"Yes. I know it sounds silly," Holly confessed, "but I've—well, I've developed a strange feeling about that chest. It scares me—like when I'm writing my story and these things nobody told me come out of the past. I can't help feeling that my chest may be something like—like Pandora's box. All the troubles in the world may fly out of it!"

"There was Hope in the bottom," Judy reminded her. "I'm willing to take the chance."

Still Holly hesitated. Cleo Potter tapped her foot impatiently. But she said nothing. Her husband, as usual, was waiting outside in the car. Holly's two sisters had gone to town with their uncle, to buy Ruth's baby a new outfit. They had taken little Billy along.

"If you're innocent, Holly," Cousin Cleo said finally, "I'll be the first to apologize."

Holly drew a deep breath. Then she said, "All right, Judy, take the chance if you want to. Wait till I call from the tunnel. Then you just push!"

And Holly ran upstairs to descend by the ladder from her uncle's room. A moment later Judy heard her muffled voice from behind the bookshelves.

"Ready?"

"All ready," Judy repeated. "What do I do now?"

"Push on the left side of the bookshelves. There! See how easily they move?"

Holly had to duck her head to keep from being hit by the bookshelves as they swung around. The sight of her crouching there beside her forbidden chest stabbed Judy's heart with pity. For a moment she almost wished she hadn't asked this favor of Holly.

"There's the chest right where she hid it," Cleo Potter pointed out.

"She only did it because it was forbidden. Her uncle understood. Help me lift it out and we'll soon discover what's in it. One look ought to convince you that Holly is innocent of these ridiculous charges you've been making against her. Close your eyes when we open it, Holly! You won't have to see a thing."

Again something rattled inside as the chest was

When the Chest Was Opened   199

lifted and returned to its original position in Holly's study. Judy had no misgivings, however, until she lifted the lid. Then she could only gasp and stare at what she saw.

"I thought so!" exclaimed Cleo Potter, pouncing upon the first thing that met her eyes.

It was the blue glass hen dish that had always tempted Holly, according to her own admission. And there it was right on top!

Nothing was broken. It must have been the cover sliding off the hen dish and rattling around in the chest that Judy had heard. She couldn't believe the evidence of her own eyes when she saw what else was there.

Wedged in between a beribboned holiday package and a stack of faded old letters was the Millville Rose!

"Holly, you didn't—" Judy began. "I was so sure you hadn't—"

But Holly was sobbing brokenheartedly, "I knew something terrible would happen if you opened the forbidden chest!"

CHAPTER XXV

A Borrowed Birthday

AT FIRST Judy could think of no word of comfort. The evidence was there and yet she simply couldn't believe it. Her heart still told her Holly was innocent.

Judy lifted and poked through the old letters, magazines, and papers that seemed to have been all Holly's mother had kept in her mysterious chest. Judy removed one of the wrapped packages and a tag fell from it. Through tears of sympathy that suddenly blurred the letters, she read:

> *To my little Christmas girl*
> *For all your birthdays* ...
> MOTHER

A Borrowed Birthday 201

Judy blinked her eyes and read the message again, the real meaning of it dawning upon her. Two of her three questions had been answered. And here, on the faded Christmas tag, was the answer to her third question: *Why was it forbidden?*

"Holly!" she exclaimed. "You were forbidden to open this chest because your mother had hidden your Christmas presents in it! Or were they your birthday presents? Anyway, she wasn't being cross or unreasonable. There wasn't anything strange about her command, the way you thought. She had just hidden these surprise packages in here and didn't want you to peek."

"And I didn't!" sobbed Holly. "I never opened the chest—not the least little crack. I didn't disobey her. But, Judy, she—she died before she could give them to me!"

It was the tragic truth. Even Cleo Potter could see it. For a moment there wasn't a sound in the room except for Holly's sobs. She was not a girl who cried easily. But this evidence of her mother's careful preparation for a Christmas that never came for her was more than Holly could take.

"I didn't intend to upset you so, Holly," her cousin began uncertainly.

"You did!" cried Holly. "You did it on purpose! You must have hidden those two pieces in there yourself!"

"Holly, what are you saying?"

"Mrs. Potter couldn't have, Holly, but surely somebody did," declared Judy. "I'm beginning to wonder—"

"What?" asked Holly, controlling her sobs a little.

"I can't tell you now," Judy said mysteriously. "But I think I can find out how this happened by simply making a telephone call. Please stand right close to the telephone and listen, Mrs. Potter," she added. "If I've figured out things correctly, you *will* have an apology to make to Holly."

The call was to the Wilcox mansion. Judy asked to speak with Harold Wilcox.

"I have a serious question to ask you," she told him. "We've just opened the forbidden chest—"

"The forbidden chest!" he exclaimed in a voice loud enough so that Cleo Potter could hear him clearly. "How did you find it?"

"Easy," Judy said. "Holly had hidden it herself, in a secret tunnel that I must show you some day. Anyway, when we opened the chest we found the blue glass hen and the Millville rose paperweight in it. And the last time I saw the Millville Rose, you were holding it in your hand!"

"I was?"

"Yes, the day you came to the Potter house in Wyville when you were selling eggs. Holly had gone into the kitchen to see if her cousins needed any, and you picked up the Millville Rose—"

"That's right, I remember," the boy interrupted. "I

A Borrowed Birthday

had taken a couple of pieces over to the window. One was a blue glass hen, and the other was the Millville Rose. You can appraise old glass better in a good light, you see, but when I heard Holly coming there wasn't time to put them back where they belonged. Naturally, I didn't want her to see me with them—"

"And so you slipped them inside the forbidden chest and turned the key! Thanks, Harold," Judy said gratefully. "That was all I wanted to know."

"Jeepers, Judy!" Harold gasped. "You never told me *those* were the things they accused Holly of taking! If I'd only known—"

"It's all right, Harold," Judy reassured him. "You couldn't possibly have known."

When she returned from the telephone, Holly had stopped sobbing, although her eyes were still red and she looked so dejected that Judy's heart ached for her. Cleo Potter's face was working strangely.

"Forgive me, Holly," she said brokenly. "I've been a fool. I should have known it wasn't you. Fred told me it wasn't, and he said even if it was, the Millville rose paperweight should rightfully have been yours, since it was left to your mother by her grandmother. Here comes Fred now," she added, wiping away something that looked suspiciously like tears. "I guess he got tired of waiting. If it's all right with him—"

When the situation was explained to him, Fred Potter said, explosively for him, "If you'll let that poor girl alone, Cleo, I'll give her the Millville Rose or anything else you want to give her. Our house has too many knickknacks in it, anyway. Come on, let's leave her in peace. The next time I drive you here it will have to be at Holly's invitation."

"I—I *will* invite you," Holly said. "And thank you, Cousin Cleo, and Cousin Fred. Only—what'll I do with such a valuable paperweight?"

"Why not keep it on your desk? Won't it inspire you to finish your story?" asked Judy when the cousins had gone.

"Those presents from my mother will inspire me more than a million paperweights," Holly declared. "They've waited so long, and one is a birthday present anyway. I *wish* my birthday didn't come on Christmas."

"Mine doesn't," Judy said. "It comes just two days from now, and Peter has already planned a party. Couldn't we trade? I'd rather like celebrating my birthday on Christmas."

"Do you mean it?" asked Holly.

"Of course."

As they talked it over, the idea of trading birthdays appealed to Holly more and more. She did want to open her present and it had to be an occasion. Judy thought it would be fun.

"I'll need an occasion myself, to tell all my adventures," she declared. "There's an awful lot I haven't

A Borrowed Birthday

told Horace. His eyes will fairly pop out of his head when he hears what a big part Peter played in the recovery of the stolen antiques. And just imagine the oh's and ah's when you show everybody the Millville rose paperweight and tell them where we found it! We'll invite Harold Wilcox, of course."

"What about asking one or two of his friends?" Holly suggested.

"Of course," agreed Judy. "I'll tell the boys Horace will call for them. He'd better, if he wants the rest of this story for his newspaper! We'll ask Al Kunkel and my young friend, Skid Keller. He will make a good partner for our little neighbor, Muriel Blade. Peter has already asked Honey and Lois and Lorraine and Arthur and I don't know how many others for my birthday. Your uncle can play, and we'll have games and dancing. It'll be quite a party!"

And so it was.

Holly had never looked prettier than she did the day of her borrowed birthday. Her cheeks were as pink as the crepe-paper streamers that crisscrossed the beamed ceiling in her uncle's big dining room. The table had been pulled out to its full length, covered with a gay cloth, and set for sixteen in honor of Holly's sixteenth birthday. But that was still a secret to many of those who had been invited.

"Happy birthday, Judy!" they called out one after another.

"But it isn't my birthday," she protested, laughing. "That's why the party is here instead of at our house. Holly and I have traded birthdays!"

"Traded birthdays!" was the general exclamation. "I never heard of such a thing—but it sounds like fun."

Finally all the guests had arrived with the exception of Horace and the boys he was bringing from Wyville. While they were waiting for them, it was decided that Holly should begin opening her presents.

"I'll leave the package from my mother until the very last," she announced, beginning to unwrap one of the packages that had been meant for Judy.

There was much merriment as Holly held up a frilly nightgown which would fit her equally as well.

A fortunetelling game was next. The whole crowd was being amused by it when Horace and the three younger boys came in.

"You know what?" Al Kunkel burst out the moment he saw Judy. "The whole club's invited to the Collector's Club dinner. We can be sort of junior members, if we want, Hal's father says. I'm bringing my collection of birds' nests."

"I've got a button collection," Skid announced.

"What are you bringing?" Holly asked when Harold was silent.

"I don't know," he began. "I—"

"Had you thought of a Millville rose paperweight? I'd just lend it to you," Holly rushed on. "Judy suggested it because of something I said about valuable things being no good unless they could be used. And Judy says it would complete your father's collection."

"Jeepers!" he said. "We can show it together. Won't Dad be surprised! Maybe Mr. Hornsby will take a picture of the collection for the Antique Journal—in color. Jeepers!"

"Who's Mr. Hornsby?" Judy asked.

"The vice-president of the Collector's Club. The president can't preside. He's in jail."

"Harold is speaking of Stanislaus R. King," Peter explained to the others. "I'm sure Mr. Wilcox's collection was next on King's list. Probably that was why he met his partner, Jack Hauser, a professional gangster posing as a wholesale antique dealer, so soon after appraising it. By the way, Judy, King and Hauser did haul the stolen antiques into New York State in the stolen car found abandoned in Olean. Remember? That was after King's own car had been wrecked.

"King was the brains of the pair," Peter went on. "He had the stuff spotted, and then Hauser committed the actual robberies. King evidently planned to incriminate Harold before stealing his father's collection, but that was a big mistake. Evidently, King thought he had Harold thoroughly cowed or he never would have risked lying about what time it was when he dropped Harold at the five-and-ten. But Harold fooled him by disappearing that same night. But let's think about something more pleasant now. Isn't that food I see on the table?"

Under the cover of the general stampede for refreshments, Holly slipped away unnoticed by anyone except Judy, to finish opening her presents.

"There's a big heavy one that I really must see," she declared. "It feels like the kitchen stove, and it's from—oh my! It has a lot of names signed to it, including yours, Judy. What can it be?"

The big present turned out to be a brand-new typewriter.

"It's for your story," Judy explained. "The Millville Rose didn't inspire you. We thought maybe this would."

"It will! Oh, what a wonderful present! Thank you, Honey, Peter, Horace, and you, too, Doris! You must all come back to my study with me afterwards and see how my beautiful new typewriter looks on my desk!"

"We want to see something else!" they clamored. "The forbidden chest!"

"You shall," Holly promised. "There isn't much in it except my mother's keepsakes—old cards and letters that are precious to me, of course, and a stack of old magazines. But you're welcome to look."

"I *have* looked," Judy said softly. "The magazines are dated in the year 1880. Does that mean anything to you, Holly?"

"It's the year of my story! It means everything!"

she exclaimed. "And now for my last wonderful present."

It was the one from her mother. Holly had saved the Christmas presents to open at the proper time, but this one was meant for her birthday.

"Oh!" she exclaimed wonderingly as she lifted the gift from its wrappings. "She *was* real!"

"Who was?" asked Judy as everyone moved closer to see what had captured Holly's attention.

It was a sampler delicately worked in a cross-stitch pattern of leaves and flowers and framed in an exquisite old frame. Above the flowers were the letters of the alphabet and below them Judy read the words: *My Garden of Happiness*. The sampler was signed *Felicity Kane*.

"She was real," Holly repeated. "She must have been my own great-grandmother, from what Cousin Cleo said. The Millville rose paperweight belonged to her."

"No wonder things came to you out of the past as you wrote your story," Judy exclaimed. "Your mother must have told you about your great-grandmother when you were very young, and Felicity's life made such an impression on you that you half remembered it."

"So that's it! And I wouldn't know yet, if you hadn't loaned me your birthday," Holly said. "Judy, I'll never forget it—not if I live to be ten times sixteen."

"That will make you a hundred and sixty!" laughed

Horace. "You won't have to write a novel to become famous if you live that long. You'll be famous just by being on earth."

And Holly answered thankfully, "It's such a good earth that I really wouldn't mind."

Judy felt that she wouldn't, either. That is, if Peter could live as long as she did. After the party, when they were on their way home, he stopped to show her the new moon and kiss her upturned face.

"Now you'll be my little Christmas girl," he said. "But darling, didn't you mind giving up your own birthday?"

"You don't give up anything when you make other people happy," she quickly protested.

And both of them knew it was true.

The dark, winding road into the mountains is only a detour—or so it seems. But what about the white-robed "ghosts" who flit about in the shadows? And how can whole truckloads of valuables disappear without a trace? These are the questions Judy and Peter set out to answer on their dangerous adventure along

THE HAUNTED ROAD

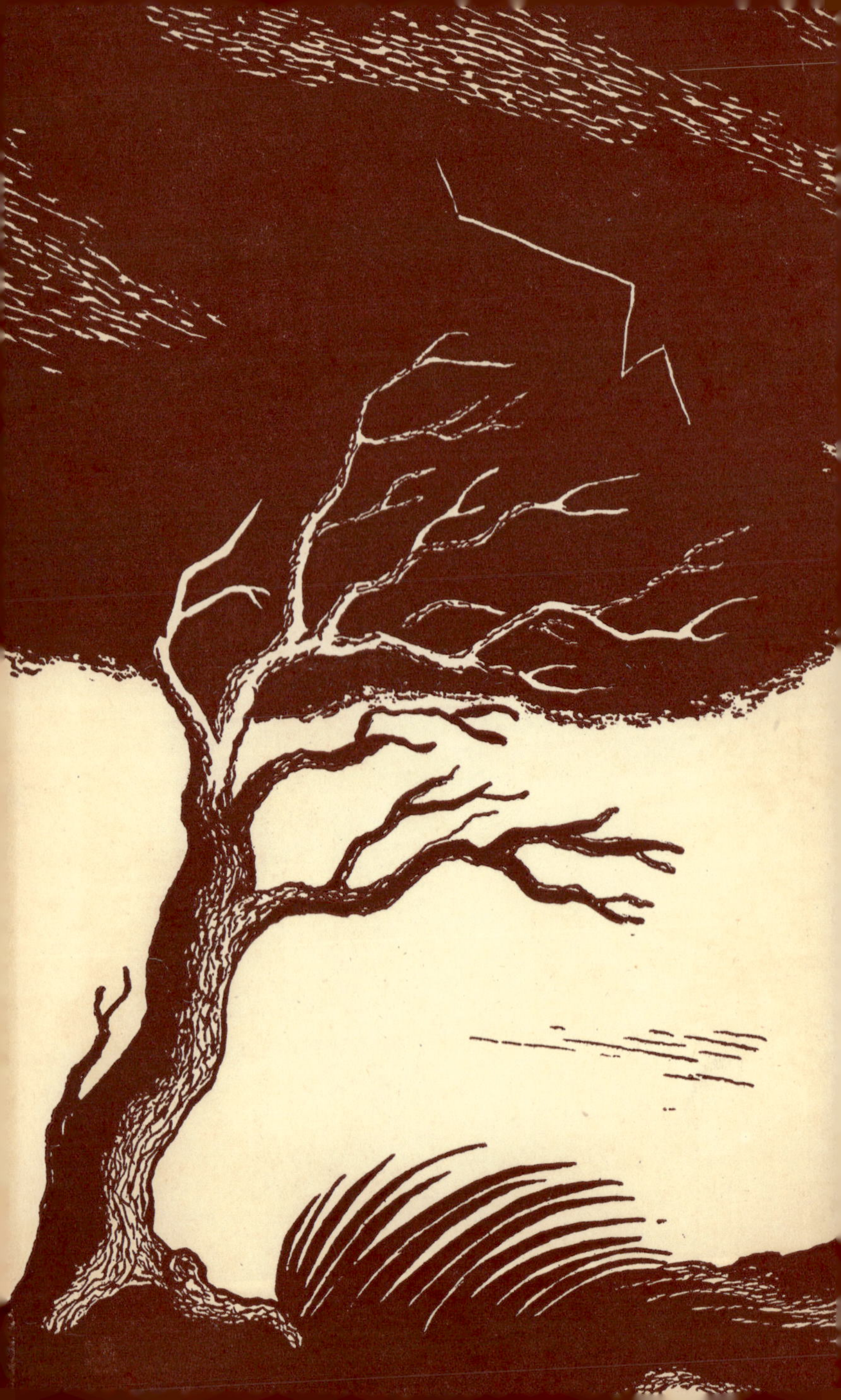